MW01252351

THEY SAY YOU CAN'T CHEAT DEATH— *well, that doesn't stop these guys from trying.*

It wasn't too hard to round up a group of unscrupulous undertakers to unearth $25,000,000 in missing cash and ice. Guys like—

JAMES DEROSSA, aka "JAMES DEAN," who came into town to mastermind the caper: *Harold & Maude.* The Feds had been watching his family since Jimmy Hoffa disappeared in 1975.

WES BISHOP & DON KING, two corrupt Crenshaw undertakers that needed the payday more than anyone else.

THE SMOTHERS BROTHERS, owners of *Coffin Depot* in West Hollywood and currently enrolled in the Funeral Rule Offenders Program. They were smothered in debt.

RAY DRISCOL, aka "QUINCY," wanted to be a celebrity coroner but never hit the big time... until now.

COFFIN JOE, hearse driver at *The Big Sleep Celebrity Death Tours.* He had encyclopedic knowledge of celebrity death and a lead foot for the getaway hearse.

Easy enough? The only problem was when Detective Hank Hellion Gladwin got in the way and started digging deeper into his LA sting operation of local funeral homes and then began connecting the dots to a cold case from Detroit in 1975 called *Operation Grim Reaper.* He knew DeRossa was involved, if only he could solve the mystery of the "*Y.*"

DEATHRYDE:

REBEL WITHOUT A CORPSE

A Novel

MICHAEL P. NAUGHTON

Gilded Hearse Press
Los Angeles, California

Copyright © 2008 by Michael P. Naughton and Gilded Hearse Press. All rights reserved.

"Deathryde: Rebel Without a Corpse"
Edited by Donna Novak

ISBN-13: 978-0-9778-6690-8
ISBN-10: 0-9778669-0-4

LIBRARY OF CONGRESS CATALOGUE
IN PUBLICATION DATA
LCCN: 2007904994
9 8 7 6 5 4 3 2 FIRST PRINTING

Gilded Hearse Press
914 Westwood Blvd. # 518
Los Angeles, CA 90024

www.GildedHearse.com

Printed in the United States

This book is dedicated to Stanley Kramer and the "big W'ya," James Bond, Slumber Inc. and Bruce Glover in Diamonds Are Forever, Robert Evans for Harold & Maude and The Kid Stays in the Picture, Ross Macdonald and his Zebra-Striped Hearse, the great Billy Wilder and Mozerella Mortuary, Jessica Mitford and The American Way of Death, and to my friend, Michael Madsen, a true rebel.

CAST OF CHARACTERS

JAMES DEROSSA, aka "JAMES DEAN" — He blew back from the past and set up the perfect crime: *Harold & Maude*. He disowned his father's funeral business. A rebel fresh out of Jackson County Jail. A rebel without a corpse.

DETECTIVE MIKE MAPLE — Still haunted by a 30 year old case called *Operation Grim Reaper*. He knew the money was still buried somewhere. But where?

DETECTIVE STAN GLEN — An FBI Agent who worked with Detective Mike Maple on *Operation Grim Reaper*. Where did he disappear to?

WES BISHOP— A Crenshaw undertaker and compulsive gambler that couldn't pass up an easy caper.

DON KING, aka "NOTORIOUS R.I.P." — He was Wes Bishop's partner in crime who suffered from highway anxiety.

THE BIG SLEEP DRIVER, aka "COFFIN JOE"— His "day-job" was showing tourists dead legends. He was a perfect front for a wheelman.

THE SMOTHERS BROTHERS: JOE & VIC — Owners of *Coffin Depot* and experts at premature burials; these guys were as crooked as they come.

DETECTIVE HANK HELLION GLADWIN — He was working overtime and connecting the dots on *Operation Coffin Nail*.

AGENT DAVID KIM — Gladwin's partner that had his doubts about *Operation Coffin Nail* and was out to nail Gladwin.

MANFRED O & GILDA HEARSE — LA Gothic vampires that wound up at the wrong place at the wrong time.

CASH WORTHINGTON — A petty criminal fresh out of Pelican Bay (he liked to stretch the truth). His Krenshaw g-sters were trailing Bishop & King.

WENDELL ROBINSON, aka "HOT POCKET" & MARK ALSTON, aka "ZIP" — Cash's posse. They were all on the highway to hell.

BELLE ISLE — A cocktail waitress at Commerce Casino and Cash's "beeitch." She tipped him off that Bishop & King were involved in something shady.

RAY DRISCOL, aka "QUINCY" — A Wayne County Coroner that held the secret to *Operation Grim Reaper*.

DAISY ACRES — The owner of a flower shop. She sent everyone the instructions for *Harold & Maude* on bouquets of sunflowers, yet experienced selective memory when questioned.

BARBARA STANWYCK — An imposter like Dean, but whose side was she really on? Who was she working for?

DEATHRYDE:

REBEL WITHOUT A CORPSE

Chapter 1.

JAMES DEAN STOOD IN FRONT OF LAX peering over his Ray-Bans as he lit an American Spirit cigarette. Of course he had been dead for over 50 years, but who was the TSA or Homeland Security to question his luggage tag.

The black town car pulled up curbside. The driver loaded Dean's bags. Dean got in. Destination: Westwood Memorial Mortuary where J.D. had to check in on some old friends: *Harold & Maude.*

At the same time retired Detroit Detective, Mike Maple, rolled three file boxes down the Southwest terminal at LAX— a Payless shoe box tucked tightly under his arm. He was Florida orange in skin tone from too many Carnival Cruises. Maple was still haunted by an unsolved case over 30 years old code-named *Operation Grim Reaper,* or OGR.

He flagged down the first blue SuperShuttle he could, loaded in and grabbed a crumpled LA Times in the seat next to him. Maple often told strangers, after he consumed a few drinks, that he was a Sky Marshall or a customs agent, depending on if he flew or took an ocean cruise. He frequently fantasized about protecting the American people. Fighting terrorism. Taking down hostile airline passengers with his sidearm. Wiretapping with George W'ya. But reality bit, and at best at the end of his road, Mike Maple was a part-time funeral home mystery shopper for the benefit of the AARP.

"Where to?" asked the SuperShuttle driver.

"11800 Wilshire," Maple said. "Federal Building in Westwood."

The SuperShuttle driver was Indian or Persian, Maple couldn't tell. He loaded Mike Maple's file boxes and carry-on and climbed back in. The driver keyed in the Westwood location on his Garmin GPS map system. He waited a few moments for other passengers and then eventually inched his way onto the 405 Freeway off of Sepulveda. They hit solid gridlock within minutes and remained mired in LA traffic as the mercury spiked, the air conditioning blasted and more fuel cooked the ozone.

Maple was claustrophobic and usually kept his mind distracted with conversation. He finally broke the ice and said, "Traffic always this bad?"

"Woorse," the driver said in a thick accent.

Maple looked around at the Angelenos flanking him in their tanks, yapping away on their cell phones— apathetic to it all. He shook his head and said, "How do people drive this everyday?"

"It drive me crazy," the driver said as he pulled out his

cell phone and rudely talked in Hindu the rest of the way, occasionally glaring at Maple in his rearview mirror.

There were some intermittent cut offs, cursing, near misses and almost rear-ended, white-knuckled, back-seat driving along the way.

Humvees. Ford Escalandes. Yukon XL's. 4Runners. All taking up twice the space. Bigger cars for even bigger assholes, Maple thought.

In LA, you are what you drive.

chapter 2.

A BLACK HEARSE WAS PARKED ON GLENDON
just outside the iron gates of Westwood Memorial Mortuary; a serene oasis tucked in the heart of Wilshire's business
district. Any dead celebrity worth their salt was interred,
inured or entombed here. This place had all the "classics."

Wes Bishop and Don King, aka "Notorious R.I.P.," had
traveled all the way from Crenshaw for this caper.

Bishop sat behind the wheel of the black hearse with
a gangster lean. He checked his watch several times. It
was now 10:25. King was always uptight and would never
drive the hearse. He asked Bishop once again, "So, how
do you know this guy again, anyway?"

"Quincy?"

"Yeah, Quincy."

"Quincy worked for the Wayne County Morgue back in
Detroit," Bishop said. "His real name is Ray Driscol, but
everyone calls 'em Quincy like that Jack Klugman dude."
Bishop laughed. "Man, what that cat wanted more than

anything else was to be a celebrity coroner like that what's-his-name?"

"Noguchi," King said.

"Yeah, Thomas Noguchi. Anyway, he got us to Dean."

They watched a silver hearse enter the gates of Westwood Memorial. The side of the hearse read: *The Big Sleep Celebrity Death Tours.*

That was their cue.

Big Sleep shuttled the morbidly curious in and out of Westwood Memorial Mortuary three times a day. Bishop and King only knew the driver as 'Coffin Joe.' He was right on time: 10:30 a.m.

Bishop shot King a look and exited the black hearse whistling Dean Martin's *Everybody Loves Somebody.*

King got out of the passenger side and slid in behind the wheel. The meter was expired.

Bishop ambled up the driveway through the gates. It was as if Sammy Davis Jr. himself was still alive. People often told Bishop he looked like Sammy, and Bishop often ate it up.

He looked across the cemetery yard; to his right was the cemetery office, and to the far left were the alcoves. He nodded to Coffin Joe as the tourists exited the *Big Sleep* hearse. Bishop then located Dean Martin's grave and the alcove labeled *Sanctuary of Love,* as he had been instructed.

There was Dino, three rows from the bottom (Born: June 7, 1917- Died: December 25, 1995). Bishop took a minute to think about *The Dean Martin Show, Matt Helm,* and martinis and then quickly plucked the fresh bouquet of sunflowers that lay at the base of the crypt.

He opened the small envelope from *Daisy Acres Floral Creations.* The front of the note read:

"Happy Birthday, Maude!"

The back read:

Hollywood Roosevelt:
8:30 P.M.
Room # 928

Bishop placed the note card in his Nehru jacket and took the bouquet of sunflowers with him. On his way out, he took a quick detour and traipsed across the lawn to locate Natalie Wood's grave. He had obviously been there before. He placed a single sunflower on her grave, dropped a post office box key in a terra cotta planter at the base of the headstone, and then high-tailed it out of Westwood Memorial and back to the hearse.

King threw open the driver's side door. He walked around the rear of the hearse. He told Bishop to drive.

"Harold & Maude opens tonight," Bishop said as he passed the note card to King, who anxiously watched a Persian woman attempt to parallel park her SUV in front of their black hearse, cursing in Farsi.

"Look at this bitch," King said. "Why would someone buy a car they can't drive?"

"You have a car you don't drive."

"That's because I don't want to get killed by people like her."

Another Ford Explorer doing an easy 70 m.p.h. blew past, nearly sideswiping the Persian SUV and swerving to avoid taking a few pedestrians with it.

Bishop commented under his breath, "Welcome to the highway arms race." He put the hearse into gear and said, "Did you hear what I said? I said Harold —"

"I heard you the first time," King said. "We gotta stop by Target and pick up a few things for Ms. Clark's wake."

"After we make a stop at the Commerce Casino," Bishop said.

"We still have a business to run."

Bishop laughed and said, "Shit, Ms. Clark ain't going nowhere."

The black hearse pulled a u-turn and headed towards Wilshire Boulevard and the 405 Freeway.

chapter **3.**

COFFIN JOE KINDLY HANDED EACH OF HIS
six looky-loo tourists a map of the Westwood Memorial
grounds from the glove compartment of the *Big Sleep*
hearse.

He was a gaunt 70's relic that donned an out-dated
Dukes of Hazard hairdo tucked under his chauffeur's cap,
an unkept bushy mustache ala Nietzsche, and wore gold
Elvis-style sunglasses. There was an uneasy, creepy vibe
about him.

"Okay folks, this is the place," he said as he checked his
watch. "We have about 20 minutes here and then it's on to
the Manson murder house on Benedict Canyon. The new
owners tore it down, but you can still get the eerie vibes."

The tourists "ooohhhed and aaaahhhhhed" and hung
on his every word of this macabre Easter egg hunt for ves-
tiges of celebrity death.

"Dominique Dunne, Jack Lemmon, Marilyn Monroe and Thurston Howell are here, lovey dears–" he said,

impersonating Jim Backus from *Gilligan's Island*. No one got his impression, which was spot on. He began walking in the opposite direction away from the *Big Sleep* hearse and the tourists. They all wanted to visit Marilyn Monroe first, of course.

"Did I say, Marilyn Monroe?" He said. "My mistake. I think she's interred at Hollywood Forever. I'll get confirmation on that... better yet, there is an office located over there." He pointed them far away from where Marilyn actually was.

One of the tourists inspected the map and assured him that Marilyn was in the direction he was headed. Coffin Joe insisted she start at the other end, blocking her path.

He walked at a brisk pace to The Corridor of Memories and ducked inside the alcove. He quickly located Crypt 24 among the wall of niches.

A Marilyn Monroe wannabe genuflected in front of the crypt of the iconic movie star (Born: Jan. 1, 1926 - Died: Aug. 5, 1962). Coffin Joe mentally calculated the current age of Ms. Monroe if she had been alive today. 82 years old. Time flies. His mind wandered for a moment wondering what she might look like now if she had lived. He snapped out of his nostalgic reverie and zeroed in on the resplendent yellow sunflowers. He was just about to reach over and snatch the bouquet when the Monroe wannabe belted out a few breathy bars of "*Happy Birthday, Mr. President.*"

Coffin Joe withdrew his hand from behind her shoulder, paused and then snatched the bouquet like a cobra. The Monroe wannabe stopped singing, looked over her shoulder and sneered at him. He smiled and turned away from her.

He glanced over at the office across the way and did not see any of his tourists. The coast was clear.

He opened up the note card from *Daisy Acres Floral Creations.* It read:

Happy Birthday, Maude!

He flipped the card over to the back. The instructions read:

Hollywood Roosevelt.

8:30 p.m.

Room # 928

Coffin Joe kissed the card, placed it back in the small envelope, put it in his pocket and blew the Monroe wannabe an airy kiss from the palm of his hand. He tipped his cap and turned into his angry group of tourists incredulously staring at him with their foldout maps. He handed one of the tourists the bouquet of sunflowers, grinning.

"Okay folks, let's get a move on. We haven't got all day," he said.

This announcement was followed by various complaints for refunds, and hemming and hawing. He managed to shepherd them back into the *Big Sleep* hearse and speed out the gates of Westwood Memorial, nearly clipping a Jag.

A black town car pulled through the gates moments later. It circled around, then stopped near the alcoves. The driver said, "Would you like to take a moment, Mr. Dean? A few moments to yourself, that is."

There was an uncomfortable silence.

The town car driver could see Dean, deep in thought, in his rear-view mirror.

"I've been here before," Dean said as he smiled. "Just wanted to see if things have changed." He motioned to the driver to move along. They took a right on Wilshire and headed eastbound to the Hollywood Roosevelt for his prearrangement conference.

All the pieces were in place.

The disinterment of *Harold & Maude* was going according to plan.

He leaned back, lit another cigarette and whistled Cat Steven's *Wild World* in between puffs.

chapter 4.

A WHITE HEARSE WAS PARKED OUTSIDE
the circular drive of the historic Hollywood Forever Cemetery in West Hollywood. Joe and Vic Smothers, known in the business as the Smothers Brothers, sat ready to roll.

"I hear they show movies here now," Vic said.

"Get outta here." Joe said.

"I'm serious. They've got some young entrepreneur that took over and he's bringing in a new crowd— a younger crowd— and introducing them to the classics. I guess they show the films on the side of the mausoleum— project the thing right onto Rudie Valley's grave. The kids are diggin' it."

"All right, let's hit it, but don't pull all the way in," J-oe said. "Hang back for a few, then go buy a postcard or something in the giftshop. I'll be a few minutes."

"No problem. I'll be right here studying for our compliance test."

"Fuck the FTC," Joe said, as he leaned back in the hearse window. "That mystery shopper that ratted on us is dead meat. It's just another reason I'm gettin' the hell out of this death racket."

"Suit yourself," Vic said. "We got busted and the Offenders Program starts next week, so I'm going regardless."

Joe walked across the lawn towards the Beth Olam Mausoleum. His footsteps echoed in the hollow, marble hallway. Joe was a macho man, solid as a brick. He hardly ever cracked a smile. It was hard to guess his ethnicity; he could look Italian or Hispanic depending on what situation you put him in. At Hollywood Forever you could project an ex-mobster onto him, given the fact he was searching for Bugsy.

He looked to his left. Three rows from the bottom was # 3087. He verified the crypt on the tourist map. There were lipstick prints all over Bugsy's tomb, but no bouquet of sunflowers. He asked himself if this was some fucking joke.

He found a groundskeeper nearby trimming some grass around a headstone. He shadowed his face from the sun and asked him in an accusatory tone, "Scuz me, our mortuary sent some sunflowers over to Bugsy... for his anniversary and you see... well, I don't see them..."

The groundskeeper had a dumb look on his face that Joe wanted to kick in.

He calmly said, "That's because a guy already picked 'em up. Said the florist made a mistake."

Joe pushed past the groundskeeper and stormed back to the white hearse. Vic was leaning on the bumper, studying. He was the opposite of his brother, a fair skinned, rangy red-head that people always mistook for Conan O' Brien. He was calm and level headed, unlike Joe.

"Get in," Joe said.

"What's wrong?"

"We got stiffed."

"What do you mean?"

"No sunflowers. No *Harold & Maude*. That bastard Quincy stiffed us."

When the Smothers Brothers got back into the white hearse, they noticed a mint, purple '67 Fleetwood hearse, with flames on the hood and side panels, driving through the gates of Hollywood Forever; it looked like it just rolled out of a George Barris showroom, customized and hot-rodded. The two gothic occupants were Manfred O, driver and unemployed trust funder, and Gilda Hearse, passenger and barrista. They were Hollywood Vampyres and those were their Goth names. At least that's what the club owner at Helter Skelter, an alternative Gothic nightclub in Hollywood, would later say. They went there often to chill— or get chilled.

Vic Smothers watched them, amused. He rubbernecked at Gilda as she exited the hearse. She was a nice package. She had milky white skin, ravenous black hair, and real breasts all poured into leather and lace. He liked her style. Manfred looked like Marilyn Manson. He had cosmetic fangs and white contacts.

They're creepy and they're kooky.

Joe's cell phone startled him when it rang. His retro ringtone was the theme from *The Munsters*.

"This is Joe," he said.

The dispassionate voice on the other end instructed:
"Move on to the next step."
"Who in the hell is this?"
Silence.
"I said, move on to the next step. The prearrangement conference is at the Roosevelt in Hollywood. 8:30 p.m. Room # 928. Don't be late."
The call disconnected.

chapter 5.

DETECTIVE HANK HELLION GLADWIN SAT behind his disheveled desk in an office on the 11th floor of the Federal Building, located in the 11800 block of Wilshire Boulevard, tracking his Amazon order on the internet. His Philips Heartstart Home Automated External Defibrillator was supposed to ship in 24 hours— "usually ships in 24 hours" it said— "usually" being the operative word. What if he experienced sudden cardiac arrest before his package arrived? It would be at Amazon's expense, he thought. He was experiencing more dull aches these days. It was also Monday and he knew that most men were at a higher risk for a heart-attack— 33% higher on Mondays. Cortisol was the culprit, so he popped a Bayer Low-Dose Chewable Orange Aspirin from his pocket. Perhaps it was the overtime on *Operation Coffin Nail,* or OCN, and a vague connection to an old case: *Operation Grim Reaper,* a convoluted 30 year old sting involving the charnel trade and some odd $25,000,000 in missing cash and ice.

The abrupt knock on the door startled him. He quickly reduced the Amazon order screen and returned to his online investigation of The Smothers Brothers' wholesale casket business in West Hollywood called *Coffin Depot*.

Agent Kim, a young, eager Korean man, sprung open the door halfway, but did not enter.

"Chief you're gonna love this one—"

"Did you get those tapes I asked for?" Gladwin barked.

"They're being transferred as we speak," Agent Kim said, grinning.

"You said that last time we spoke." Gladwin stood up irritated, rubbing his neck.

"I got something else you'll be interested in."

"I'm interested in those tapes, Mr. Kim. I've got a ton of work to finish here on these LA Funeral Home sweeps— for chrissakes, it's bad enough we spend our whole life getting shystered, then we die and we've got these grave digging bastards robbing us at the end of our road..."

Kim knew the Gladwin rants quite well and interjected: "It's a link in the investigation, G-man."

Gladwin liked being called 'G-man.' It made him feel like Cagney or some other Hollywood throwback. He softened:

"A link in OCN?"

Kim opened the door wider to reveal: Mike Maple.

Maple rolled in his file boxes and took a seat in front of the cluttered desk. He took the shoe box from under his arm and gently placed it on the leather seat next to him.

Maple noted the health conscious reads stacked on the far right corner of the desk: *Fit for Life, The 8-Week Cho-*

lesterol Cure Cookbook, Dr. Atkin's New Diet, The Zone, and various other titles by holistic guru Andrew Weil.

"Would you like some green tea," Gladwin said as he steeped a new bag from underneath the nozzle of the Arrowhead water cooler.

"Do you have any coffee?" Maple asked.

"'Fraid not," Gladwin said as he took a seat and pulled a file from a stack of papers. "They say green tea is better for you anyway."

Maple sat there staring at Detective Gladwin for several minutes. Gladwin was large in stature, nearly 6'4, chiseled and grizzled.

"First off, Detective Gladwin, it's a pleasure to meet you—"

Gladwin was never one for proprieties. He cut Maple off and said, "So what brings you out to California?"

Maple said, "I have been doing some work for the AARP."

He opened up one of the file boxes and handed Gladwin a report from one of his most recent visits to a local funeral home. Gladwin glanced at it superficially and said, "Yes, I see, you did a little mystery shopping."

"Most of the mortuaries were clean and fully compliant with the FTC Funeral Rules."

"Most?" Gladwin leaned back in his chair and studied Maple's face.

"A few didn't disclose prices, but we caught 'em. They agreed to participate in the Funeral Rules Offenders Program and pay the fine to the U.S. Treasury Department."

Gladwin said, "They say you can't cheat death—

well, that doesn't stop these guys from trying."

Maple wasn't sure whether or not Gladwin was making a joke. He shifted in his seat and explained, "When Agent Kim contacted me regarding the surveillance tapes from Operation Grim Reaper... of course I wanted to bring them down in person and meet with you, having worked the case... I mean, anything I can do to assist..."

Gladwin grinned and said, "Of course."

He glanced at the Coffin Depot website and clicked on his discount casket of choice. "I've been doing a little mystery shopping myself," Gladwin said as he turned on the antiquated TASCAM tape deck with its two revolving tape reels marked: OGR-29SEP75

Intermittent statements masked in static played:

"Tutor..." "beautiful bouquet..." "cash at the Y," and *"55..."*

Click. Rewind. Replay several times.

Gladwin shut off the tape and got out of his chair. He looked down on the lumbering noon traffic of Westwood Boulevard and out towards UCLA.

"Y'know, I've coordinated a lot of interesting sting operations over the course of my career— everything from terrorism to music piracy. Arabs plotting bombings, to college kids ripping music— from the innocuous to the iniquitous— I have seen it all. And just when I've thought I've seen it all, I see a case like this."

Gladwin sat back down and switched on the tape again and said, "I gotta tell you, this case fascinates me."

He replayed the same phrases over and over again.

Click. Rewind. Replay.

"Tutor..." *"beautiful bouquet..."* *"cash at the Y,"* and *"55..."*

"Cryptic. Six hundred hours of conversation. Thousands of leads. Six months of wire taps and it ends there—right before your guy was ejected."

Gladwin turned to look at Maple whose eyes were squeezed shut, his hands steepled in front of his mouth.

"Detective Gladwin," Maple said, "you ever had a tune run through your head and you just can't chase it out?"

"Yeah, I've been hearing a theramin the minute I opened this investigation."

Maple said, "Every time I hear those tapes... it still chills me to this day."

Gladwin was touched. Not really.

Mike Maple's mind flashed back to the OGR stakeout in 1975 when he and his partner, Detective Stan Glen, parked across the street from DeRossa & Sons Mortuary and surveillanced the wake from a local Dairy Queen.

Maple said, "You have to understand, this was just after Jimmy Hoffa had disappeared from the Machus Red Fox restaurant in Detroit. The Feds were on hyperalert. Everyone was suspect. Operation Grim Reaper was initiated when we were tipped off that Big Frank DeRossa, the owner of the Mortuary, could've been disposing of guys like Hoffa and using the business as a front."

He recollected how Stan sat there eating his parfait on the side of the Dairy Queen on that dismal, Detroit night. "We sent our undercover guy into the wake at approximately 7:15 p.m. The decedent was a Russian guy named Ivan Illych. No history on the guy. Closed casket. Bad car accident. The wake was a mixture of Italians and Russians. He was good on the inside... for maybe 20 minutes, until DeRossa's goons caught onto him— static was all we heard over the RF Transmitter for the longest time."

Maple sat thinking about the intermittent swish of the wiper blades and the glimpses of attendees going in and out of DeRossa & Sons Funeral Home that night.

Gladwin sat there with no expression on his face, not saying a word.

Maple grinned and said, "I'll never forget Stan's annoying joke in the midst of that stakeout. Would you like to hear it?"

Gladwin nodded and went back to tracking his order on Amazon, half-listening.

Maple went on, "It went something like: There's this Jersey lawyer, a used car salesman and a banker gathered at a friend's casket." He paused, thinking. "Maybe it was a Jersey banker, a lawyer and a used car salesman, anyway... In his grief the banker says, 'In my family we have a tradition of giving the dead some money so they'll have some to spend in the afterlife...' shoot, I think it's supposed to be the next life..."

Gladwin was now surfing the web Googling for symptoms. He typed in heart palpitations and interrupted:

"Who gives the dead money?"

Maple said, "The banker says that... about their— his family tradition..."

"Ohh," Gladwin moaned as Maple continued. "So the banker drops a c-note in the casket. The used car salesman drops another hundred and the lawyer... the dickless bastard— those were Stan's words— takes out the bills, pockets the money and writes a check for three hundred dollars." Maple slapped his knee and chortled.

"So this happened that night?" Gladwin said, seriously.

Maple cleared his throat and said, "Okay, so our undercover guy came back to the car. We passed him the mug shot book to see if he recognized any of the attendees."

"Did he?"

"No," Maple said, "but here's the interesting thing. What he did see, right before he was ejected, was that Big Frank DeRossa slipped his little son, James, the Memorial Guest Registry book.

"So?"

"So, the first book wasn't filled up. Why swap it out?"

"Maybe that was it for guests that evening."

"Not hardly."

"Maybe the book got damaged."

"I highly doubt it. Look Detective Gladwin, DeRossa knew he was being surveillanced." Maple sat on the edge of his seat watching Gladwin closely. He raised his voice. "That book is the key to where the money and diamonds are buried, that's always been my theory. It's like the Maltese Falcon in this unsolved case."

Gladwin laughed and said, "This is a much stranger bird."

Gladwin got up and walked over to a cemetery map pinned on the wall, riddled with black stickpins; it resembled the map from the movie with Richard Boone, *I Bury the Living*. He studied it for a moment stroking his chin. "What makes you think the money and diamonds are buried anyway?"

"It's their business," Maple said. "Where else would it be stashed?"

Gladwin didn't answer, he just stood ruminating on the wall map. He finally said, "Humor me: Is Jimmy Hoffa a fender, a hub cap or both?"

Maple didn't get the gist of this question.

"Scuz me?"

"Is Hoffa a fender, hub cap or both?"

"There's one theory, that he is part of Giant Stadium–that he was thrown into a car. Crushed. Smelted and then crammed into a fifty-five gallon drum and hauled off by a Gateway transportation truck to an undisclosed location—"

"I didn't ask that. I asked you what you thought."

"Look Detective Gladwin, he could be *Soylent Green* for all I care. Some of us in the department speculated that Hoffa became a Renaissance man."

"Renaissance man?"

"Yeah, they built the RenCen in Detroit around the time that Hoffa disappeared. The Cosa Nostra had ties with various cement companies... well, use your imagination, who knows."

Maple pulled a file from one of the file boxes next to him. He handed Gladwin a black and white photo from White Chapel Cemetery in Michigan and said, "The money and jewels are buried somewhere out at White Chapel in Detroit."

"That's where your investigation ended."

"Yes. A dead-end."

"So you say."

Maple noticed a large concentration of pins at Hollywood Forever. He got up from his seat and stood next to Gladwin, who stood scrutinizing the map.

"Oh, this is way off base, Detective Gladwin. The money never made it out of White Chapel."

Gladwin examined Maple's face for a moment, then said, "Are you aware that Frank's son, James DeRossa, was released from Jackson County earlier this month?"

"Of course, it's big news back in the Motor City," Maple said. He handed Gladwin the article from the Detroit News.

"DeRossa just finished serving a 25 year sentence for second-degree murder."

"And didn't say one word to anybody about anything," Maple said. "He served his time."

Maple pulled out another photo from his file box. Gladwin examined the black and white photo of a charred hearse in a rain-soaked parking lot. He had seen the photo before. Only the framework and chassis were distinguishable. This was Big Frank's hearse and Big Frank was the driver.

"The Russians did that." Maple said.

"And James did this."

Gladwin passed Maple another graphic black and white photo of a bombed out autoshop which was really a Russian chop shop. He said, "James DeRossa is out and my guess is that he's not looking to start a new life in the funeral business."

"Who knows," Maple said.

Gladwin replayed the tape: *"Tutor..."* *"beautiful bouquet..."* *"cash at the Y,"* and *"55"*...

"Did Big Frank know anyone at the local Y?" Gladwin said.

"The Y?"

Gladwin did a sarcastic gesticulation of the Village People's YMCA with his arms.

Maple laughed and said, "No, I don't think it's hidden there, but we never thought of investigating the YMCAs and tearing up a gymnasium or swimming pool."

Gladwin shuffled some papers and then sat on the edge of his desk, suggesting it was time for Maple to leave.

"I'd like to get your partner's side of the story from that night," he said. "We're having trouble locating him."

"Stan Glen?" Maple said.

"Yeah, I'd like to pool him in, put him in the loop."

Maple stared down at the Payless shoe box, his eyes welled up with tears for a moment. He fought back the emotions, then carefully removed a gold Grecian urn.

"We got so busy talking..." he stammered. "Part of my coming out here was to scatter my partner over the Pacific. He never got a chance to retire."

Gladwin grimaced at the urn.

Stan Glen was ashes.

He didn't know what to say.

"Ah sure, that's a good thing... I suppose we could get more info by other means... send for it— have it sent to us."

"I'm headed to Catalina," Maple said, "It's what Stan Glen wanted."

"Catalina is a beautiful resting place. I can put you in touch with some folks down there."

"That won't be necessary," Maple said as he slowly rose from his chair and respectfully cradled the Payless shoe box.

Gladwin showed him to the door. He grabbed a book from the nearby stack and handed it to Maple on his way out. It was a copy of Leo Tolstoy's *The Death of Ivan Illych*.

"DeRossa buried a fictional character," Gladwin said with a shit-eating grin, "but I'm sure your department was up on Russian literature."

"Of course." Maple said, taking slight offense at such a major detail. He walked out the door and did not turn back.

Gladwin watched him walk down the hallway and slowly closed the door. He returned to the tape deck and hit "play."

"Cash at the Y." Stop. Rewind. *"Cash at the Y"* Stop. Rewind. *"Cash at the Y."*

He picked up the phone and instructed Agent Kim to gather all interstate records of Michigan remains that were forwarded to the state of California between '74 – '75.

He then hung up, hesitated for a moment, ruminating and then placed a call to the Wayne County Health Department in Michigan.

Chapter 6

CASH WORTHINGTON STOOD AT THE entrance of the Commerce Casino, a free man. Just released from LA County Jail. If you didn't know Cash, he would bullshit you and tell you he did time in the SHU: Pelican Bay Security Housing Unit— It was true that he was one strike away from doing some serious time, but not in the SHU.

The LA County prosecutor cut him a good deal this last time around for a B & E at a local liquor store and felt sorry for him because Cash was, himself, the victim of a botched drive-by that left him with a permanent limp and a colostomy bag. This was his welcome home party. His Krenshaw Mafia, spelled with a capital "K," had seen their killing spree heyday. The only two living sidekicks he had left were Mark Alston, aka "Zip," and Wendell Robinson, aka "Hot Pocket." Together, they were just three badass dudes, chillin' in their do-rags and Tommy Hilfiger designer clothes, looking to roll some high rollers.

Wendell and Zip debated endlessly about the Tupac murder and wielded Oliver Stone-like government conspiracy theories.

Zip was convinced that the government killed Tupac and no one could tell him otherwise. He picked up the coup d'état phrase from Oliver Stone's JFK film. He even referred to drive-bys as coups d'état.

It annoyed the shit out of Cash.

Wendell grabbed the glass door. The posse swaggered through.

"The government can kills anyone they wants to," Zip said.

"How you figure?" Wendell said.

" 'Cause they got that Patriot Missile Act and shit–says they can."

"Government sheeeeeiiit," Wendell said, "Tupac wasn't fucking JFK and if he was, then Biggie is Oswald, plain and simple. No grassy knoll shit. It was gangsta shit, not government shit.

"Yeah, well since Biggie was the size of that grassy knoll," Zip said, "then how you gonna explain to me that nobody done seen his big ass that night?"

Wendall was at his wits' end. Cash was limping ahead of them, checking out the action in the casino.

Wendall said, "Biggie sure got his, but it still don't make sense."

"Okay brainiac," Zip said, "answer me this: then who is Biggie's Jack Ruby?"

Wendell was stumped on that one. He yelled to Cash.

"Cash?" He said. "Do you think the government killed Tupac?"

Cash pivoted back around, grabbing a drink off the tray of a waitress walking past him. He said, "You think I'm tellin' you suckas? I got the whole story in the pen right after they killed Orlando Anderson and I'm takin' it to my GA-rave."

They walked through the Assyrian/Babylonian architecture with its imported plants, cascading waterfalls and shaded walkways. Cash's longtime girl, Belle Isle, was busy serving a round of drinks in the craps area. She was built like Beyonce with cornrowed hair. They threw down their pocket change. Belle smacked Cash on the lips. He smacked her on the ass. She laughed and said, "You sittin' at the wrong table, tiger."

They shifted their gaze to Bishop and King playing a few hands of California Lowball. Bishop was playing. King was still ranting. Cash was all ears.

"Tell me 'mo," he said.

"They regulars," Belle said, "At least the Sammy Davis dude is. This is the first time I seen the other cat. Sammy keeps calling him 'Notorious R.I.P.'"

They all looked at Bishop and King with a sidelong glance.

"Man, that's disrespectful." Cash said. He looked at Wendell and Zip, his nostrils flaring and gold tooth gleaming. Neither one of them had to be mind readers to know Cash was thinking of rolling them. They knew the look.

They observed Bishop. He kept folding more times than the hotel maid. The dealer kept taking his money and King kept ranting louder. They were able to make out that something was going on at the Roosevelt Hotel.

Belle went back over to eavesdrop with another round of drinks. Bishop had ordered King a Jack and Coke to take the edge off.

"We'll hit the Roosevelt after a few more hands," Bishop said.

"Speaking of dead presidents, where'd you get the big bills from?" King said.

Bishop lied. "I sold a few caskets to one of them Reality TV shows, *Fear Factor* or some shit like that."

"Always highfalutin, Wes." King relented, "You know, I'm not the only one with this problem..."

"What problem?" Bishop said.

"The freeways," he said. "I was reading about Stanley Kubrick, the guy that did *Clockwork Orange*. He wouldn't allow his driver to go over 35 m.p.h."

"Good, you got him beat by 10 m.p.h."

King knew he was just making excuses. He traced his anxiety disorder back to his youth: For one, he had an over-protective mother that told him to stay off "those dangerous freeways" and reinforced his fear— One time when he was a kid, she took him to a matinee of the film *Chitty Chitty Bang Bang*. He was afraid of flying too, so a flying car was terrifying and sent him screaming out of the movie theater. His mom said it was okay for Donny to be afraid. Secondly, he actually was in a bad accident. He flipped his Jeep Cherokee back in '82 on the I-94 in Detroit. He was lucky he crawled out alive, but never really got over his highway anxiety. He always felt crazy when he got behind the wheel, like he wanted to crash into the guard rail. He got severe panic attacks and avoided freeways any chance he could. He rationalized: on the one hand, that big SUVs were good for undertakers and sent a lot of business their way. On the other hand, these trucks were killers and caused a lot of carnage. He agreed with Ralph Nadar that they were "unsafe at any speed." He wondered if consumers knew that undertakers once used Suburbans as hearses back in the '80s. GM engineers designed the Suburbans with that in mind. Its measurements were exact specs for coffins and body bags.

Ah, the evolution of a killing machine: the Jeep became the SUV and the SUV became the Humvee. Those slick car commercials fueled by Led Zeppelin's *Rock & Roll* never featured a mangled driver on a slab at the morgue; the more appropriate song for those commercials would be *Stairway to Heaven*. King swore that before he met G-O-D the last thing in life he wanted to see was G-M-C and it's gargantuan grill guard taking his head off.

"Look Don, you want my advice," Bishop said. "You're just like a dog. It's car sickness or motion sickness. Take a Dramamine or see a shrink."

Belle looked repulsed during the whole story and kept looking over her shoulder trying to break away. Finally she made a pointless remark:

"So you work on dead people."

"Not for long," Bishop said. "My partner and I are coming into a whole helluva a lot of money and we're also sellin' off our business for a hefty six, seven figures and I'm heading to Paris to live and die like Screamin' Jay Hawkins, a happy man. I think the only thing missin' is you."

King had to wretch at those cheap pickup lines. Who was he kidding? They were both in up to their necks in debt. The IRS had a lien on everything they owned and they had paid out several times on decedent lawsuits. *Harold & Maude* was their only ticket out of this mountain of debt. Belle was a peach out of reach. Bishop needed to get real and stick to the low hanging fruit in the strip clubs in Crenshaw after a hard day at the mortuary. Those coke whores were as zombied out as the decedents they worked on and could never hear above the rap music to know that Bishop was an undertaker.

Bishop squeezed $300 in Belle's hand and kissed her on the cheek.

"We're sorta gangsters, you could say."
Belle cocked her head and gave Bishop a reproving raised eyebrow look.

"Gangstas?" she said.

"The real deal," Bishop said. He could see Belle's wheels were turning; he was just too stupid to see that he was under them.

She excused herself and went back to report this to the real g-sters sitting nearby. Zip and Wendall were still wielding Tupac conspiracy theories.

"Cash baby," Belle said.

"Whatchu want?" he said.

"Those dudes claim they's ganstas," she said.

They all looked across at the table where Bishop and King sat, then looked at each other and laughed their asses off. Belle wasn't laughing.

"I'm serious, baby," she said, "I think they got somethin' big goin' on. Sammy Davis can't keep he eyes off me. I think I can pump him fo' mo' info— His partner ain't sayin' shit and flashin' him looks which makes me think it the truth. I mean, y'know I hear lottsa brothers talk lottsa shit 'round these tables, but I think Sammy can't keep his mouth shut, y'know what I'm saying? He tryin' his hardest to hook my interest..."

Cash said, "He looks like he's been hit with the ugly stick."

"Still, I gotta say my instinct is good on this one, baby," Belle said as she pursed and glossed her lips.

Cash sat there for a long time ruminating about his third strike and how he was just born bad, and how the world would have to deal with his wrath and how he wanted that world, like Al Pacino in *Scarface*. It was destiny that these two brothers crossed his path and he was going to take it away from them.

Chapter 7

DEAN SAT ON THE EDGE OF THE BED IN HIS black Zegna suit nursing a scotch on the rocks and watching *Diamonds Are Forever,* the seventh James Bond film in the series that brought Sean Connery back as 007— *the only 007,* Dean thought. The scene played where Bond gets picked up by the hoods in the Slumber, Inc. hearse at the airport. Dean was amused.

The first knock on the door came from Coffin Joe, followed by the Smothers Brothers and finally Bishop and King— 15 minutes late.

Dean reminded them.

"You're 15 minutes late."

King flashed Bishop a nasty look.

They entered the room, made their introductions and the meeting got underway at 8:45 p.m.

Dean pulled out various items from his black leather bag: maps, permits, expo tickets and photos. Coffin Joe slipped him a bulging copy of *Mortuary Management* magazine. Dean winked at CJ, then pulled a .357 Magnum from inside the magazine. He pivoted the gun around the room and said, "In Detroit we have a saying: *Nobody moves, nobody gets hurt...*"

Everyone froze in their seats. Dean paused, then slowly lowered the Magnum. He laughed and said, "My father used to tell his customers the same thing."

Everyone except Joe got the joke.

"All right, let's get the show on the road," Dean said.

Joe Smothers said, "Wait a minute, shouldn't we wait for Quincy?"

"No, I sent 'em to look for Peter Lawford... he'll be a while."

The room broke into laughter again, with the exception of Joe Smothers. Vic got the joke and was laughing at Joe who had a stupid look on his face.

"Did I miss something?" Joe said.

Coffin Joe said, "Yeah, Lawford's ashes were scattered at sea."

Joe Smothers was still confused.

Coffin Joe went on and said, "Okay, okay maybe we shouldn't be laughing here. You do remember poor Peter from the Rat Pack, right?" He paused.

Joe Smothers nodded yes.

"Well, he couldn't afford the rent at Westwood Memorial, so his widow removed his urn— James Spada talks about it in his biography on Lawford."

Dean was studying Joe Smothers carefully at this point, which Joe took note of and then began to feign understanding.

"Yeah, poor Peter, I got it," Joe said. He forced a laugh and nudged Vic Smothers, who was now fixated on *Diamonds Are Forever*.

Coffin Joe continued, "Anyway, his widow invited the *National Enquirer* for a photo op when she scattered his ashes. That's the short version. Tell you what, I'll comp you a ride on the Big Sleep tour and tell you all about it... I've got tons of stories."

It was apparent that Joe Smothers did not like Coffin Joe. He stared at his disheveled hair and Elvis shades. He just thought Coffin Joe was a loser.

Bishop chimed in with some Dean Martin lyrics singing: *"Ain't that a kick in the head?"*

King could smell the heavy liquor on Bishop and wondered who else could.

Dean proceeded to hand out three manila envelopes to the group. He said, "All right, let's talk marble cities," and removed the mirror over the desk to reveal a map of Ascension Cemetery in Orange County.

Dean pulled out several old news clippings circa 1975 from the Detroit Free Press and passed them clockwise around the room. Some noteworthy headlines read: *"Pirates of the Columbarium: Detroit Funeral Business Still Hiding Treasure Island from Authorities"* and *"Detroit Undertaker, Under Suspicion."*

"My father knew some of the best spin doctors in the Motor City that could send even Columbo barking up the wrong Maple tree— he paid off local reporters— none of these stories amounted to squat and turned up zilch on the missing loot. They traced it to White Chapel Memorial in Troy Michigan, but the trail went cold."

Dean drew a serpentine line from Ascension, marked "Point A" on the map, to the Anaheim Convention Center, marked "Point B." He then handed out several expo tickets, again clockwise.

"These are your tickets to the Seventy-fifth NMA: National Morticians Association tradeshow, or Death Expo as I like to call it. The Death Expo is our rendezvous and opens on Friday morning." He took a sip of scotch and then went on. "Phase one: Bishop and King have the first pickup in their black hearse."

Dean handed them an envelope stamped by the State Department of Health.

King opened the envelope and authenticated the Disinterment Permit. It was the real deal. He was impressed. Yes, Dean has friends in high places.

"I pulled some strings at the County Registrar's office," Dean said. "Now, when you guys enter the gates of Ascension, the only person on duty will be a superintendent. He's a plant. You show him the permit. He opens the pearly gates. Got it?"

Dean drew the line past the El Toro "Y" and marked an "X" near the exit.

"Let's face it, the Feds stink at Algebra. X + Y = $. They still think the money is interred at White Chapel in Michigan. They're off course by at least 3,000 miles."

King said, "Ascension is fifteen miles southeast of Disneyland near the El Toro Y."

"Yes," Dean gave him a concerned look and said, "And your point is?"

King did not reply. He started obsessing about the freeway.

Dean turned to the Smothers Brothers and said, "Did you get the dummy caskets?"

"Check." Joe said confidently.

"Good. Now after Bishop and King pull in, The Smothers Brothers will pull in approximately 5 minutes later in their white hearse."

"You still haven't told us where the crypts are," Joe said.

"Uh-ah... not so fast. You won't know that until the morning of the heist. The superintendent has further instructions for you on bouquets of sunflowers."

Dean transferred two black Memorial Guest Registry books from his briefcase to his black leather bag. He drew another line on the map, just past the "Y," and circled "Point C."

"After *Harold & Maude* have been located, Bishop and King will exit Ascension. They will then escort *Harold & Maude* to 'Point C,' Trabuco Road by Lake Forest— there is a vacant tract of land there— The Smothers Brothers will trail behind and do what my father used to call a little Batesville and switch with the dummy caskets."

"For chrissakes." Joe said as he stood up.

"Scuz me?" Dean said.

"I mean, it's nonsense. Why not switch *Harold and Maude* at Ascension. Skip that step. You're joking, right?"

"Did Sean Connery polish coffins as a kid?"

"I don't know? Did he?" Joe looked around the room. Coffin Joe nodded yes.

"Good," Dean said, "so we make the switch at Trabuco Road. That copy of the reinterment permit must be affixed to the outside of the casket. If you get stopped by any cops along the way, you just tell them you are en route to Cypress View Mausoleum in San Diego. All the paperwork checks out."

Joe continued to glare at the slovenly Coffin Joe who placidly sat in the corner with his Elvis shades on.

"I still don't get what this joker's part is in all this?" Joe said jerking his thumb at Coffin Joe.

"Joker?" Dean said. "He's the best wheelman in the business. He'll be trailing both of you. If the CHP stops either of you, Coffin Joe has been instructed to blow past the boys— sort of a crash coach, if you will. That will lead them on a steeple chase. Make the Breaking News."

Coffin Joe gesticulated stepping on the gas and shifting air. He sat back smug, grinning ear to ear at the foot Joe just inserted into his own mouth.

The room fell silent.

King kept shifting in his seat, ready to bolt from the room. His anticipatory anxiety was mounting. High speed chases flickered through his mind. He looked at Dean and said, "Police don't jack around anymore with pursuits. They're sick of it. They've got spike strips, pit maneuvers and all kinds of shit, so I don't care if he's *The Road Runner, Mad Max, Bandit* or *Bullitt*. He's better off dead if he gets caught, and if he survives, the cops will beat the livin' shit out of him and then he'll do hard time."

"Nobody's getting caught." Dean assured.

Coffin Joe said, "Hey, I'm just going the extra mile for a tourist."

"And who is your tourist?" King asked.

"I am." Dean said.

He then drew a line to the Anaheim Convention Center perimeter and then to the back gate.

"Finally, the Smothers Brothers will pull around back of the convention center and meet CJ and me. There will be a vendor there by the name of Gilded Hearse. *Harold & Maude* will remain there until load out, and then we'll split everything up."

Dean calmly took a sip of his scotch and ruminated on the Rat Pack for a moment. He smiled whenever he remembered Sinatra.

"If all goes according to plan, we walk into the NMA trade show, collect some business cards, browse the tools of our past profession, and then have a nice afterlife."

The meeting ended at 9:30 p.m. Coffin Joe and Bishop and King gathered their plans and left.

The Smothers Brothers were about to exit when Dean closed the door in front of them.

"Gentlemen, sit down... what's the big rush?" He walked back over to the Magnum and glanced back at Joe.

"So how's F.R.O.P?" Dean said.

"What can I say," Joe said, "it's sorta like a traffic school for undertakers— so we made an illegal left hand turn."

James took out a photocopy of a court pleading from his briefcase and looked it over and said, "Charging $40K for a casket and then another $50K for mausoleum space is no left hand turn."

"Okay, it's more like we blew a red light."

"More like reckless driving while intoxicated and a few red lights."

Dean glanced back to *Diamonds Are Forever*. Bond was on the deck of the cruise liner with Tiffany Case, played by Jill St. John. He thought St. John was hot. He thought so as a kid and still did. Bond just flipped Mr. Wint overboard with the bomb between his legs.

Dean began placing the documents and maps back into his bag.

"Quincy highly recommended you guys," Dean said. "I won't hold your lack of celebrity death trivia against you. The real question remains: how fast can we wash the money after *Harold & Maude* are disinterred?"

Joe did some quick mental calculations and said, "Lemme give it to you in movie terms."

"Sure, I already checked the room for bugs. It's clean, go ahead."

"Post-production... say two weeks tops to edit this restorated release."

"I'm in town for one. Make it one week."

Vic could see Dean was just pushing Joe's buttons. He kept his mouth shut. Joe was imploding.

Joe said, "Hey wait a minute, restoration takes time. We agreed on two weeks. We agreed on that when we initially talked to Quincy."

Dean took another sip and turned off the TV.

"Well, you guys are restorative artists," he said. "One week or you drop 2% in your commission."

Vic Smothers attempted to ease the tension between Joe and Dean and threw in a non sequitur comment. He said, "So have you seen Montgomery Clift's ghost in this room?"

Joe Smothers looked at his brother wondering what the hell he was talking about.

Dean put his hand on Vic's shoulder and said, "This place is filled with ghosts... that's why I chose it."

He winked at them both.

The Smothers Brothers looked at each other. They left even more tense than before and a little spooked to boot.

DEATHRYDE: REBEL WITHOUT A CORPSE

Chapter **9**

THE SMOTHERS BROTHERS WALKED THROUGH
the crowded lobby of the Hollywood Roosevelt Hotel.
Someone tipped off the paparazzi that Paris Hilton was using the bathroom there, and they descended like flies. Joe
and Vic jostled their way through the looky-loos and hack
photographers.

"I'm seeing fucking white spots," Joe said. "It's gonna trigger a damn migraine... I can feel it comin' on." He shoved
one of the paparazzi out of the way, and handed the valet
his ticket at the window.

Vic was amused by all the hoopla. He said, "You wanna
hang around and grab a bite at the Dakota?"

"No," Joe said, "I'd like to throw a tent over this circus
and get the fuck out of here— and what the hell was that
load of crap about Marty Cliff?"

"Montgomery Clift."

"Whoever." Joe didn't like to be corrected.

"People claim that room is haunted," Vic said.

"People are full of shit," Joe said, which was his general philosophy. He directed the comment at the valet as the valet took his ticket.

They proceeded to walk outside the Roosevelt and wait for their white hearse.

"I'm gettin' a migraine, here it comes," Joe said. He lit a cigarette and impatiently waited for their hearse, which seemed like twenty minutes. He wondered briefly if Paris Hilton damaged any cars in the parking lot.

"Dean is onto us," Vic said. "I mean, the guy didn't just fall off a turnup truck."

Joe was focused on the valet and white spots.

Joe's cell phone rang. It was the Munsters ring tone again.

"Yeah?"

"Did you see it?" The voice on the other end asked.

"Yeah... both of 'em."

"Both?" The voice was irritated.

"You heard what I said. I saw two black Memorial Guest Registry books."

There was a long silence on the other end.

"Are you still there?" Joe said.

The voice on the other end finally answered, "One is a red herring— has to be."

"Dean wouldn't say shit about the..." The voice cut him off and said, "We've got him on our radar, no worries." The call disconnected.

The valet finally pulled up with their white hearse. Joe took a long, hard look at the scratch on the front bumper in between the fading white spots of camera flashes. He looked at the valet who said, "Don't look at me," and swore up and down the scratch was there when they parked it. Vic nudged him not to make a scene or draw attention to themselves in front of the Roosevelt. Joe complied, but argued all the way back to Coffin Depot that it was probably that Paris Hilton bitch, and with all her goddam money she didn't even have the decency to leave a note offering to fix it.

Chapter **10**

BISHOP AND KING WALKED DOWN HAWTHORNE
Avenue just a few blocks away from the Hollywood Roosevelt. They parked there to save a few bucks since Wes,
thinking with his dick, had to leave Ms. Belle Isle a $300
tip. He was now officially out of cash until he hit an ATM,
and was still no closer to a romp with Ms. Isle.

"So why wasn't Quincy there?" King said.

"Don't know." Bishop said.

King knew there was more to the story. There always was
with Bishop. If Bishop didn't have a story, then he had a
secret and the secret was going with him to his grave. Like
Bishop's Screamin' Jay Hawkins story. King had heard it
hundreds of times about how Bishop owes his whole un-
dertaking career to Screamin' Jay Hawkins, the legendary
50's soul singer that "put a spell" on Bishop as a teenager.
It was about the day he'll never forget when Screamin' Jay
came into his father's mortuary to purchase some caskets
for his stage show. Screamin' Jay pulled up in his zebra-

striped hearse with his entourage, donning his silk cape and conk hairdo— which was really why Bishop still greased his afro, not because of Sammy Davis. Screamin' Jay was not like today's bald rappers who have no sense of theater, just hostility. But Bishop's father bought into the fear of the religious groups and local undertakers, urging folks to refuse rentals of caskets for Screamin' Jay's stage show and Bishop's pop said "no way in hell" to Screamin' Jay— that it was sacrilegious. But young and impressionable Wes Bishop talked to Screamin' Jay outside and arranged a back door deal when his father was picking up a corpse later that evening. Screamin' Jay's zebra-striped hearse came rolling through the alley and they covertly loaded a casket in the back of it and Bishop got an open ended backstage pass to all of the concerts any time Screamin' Jay rolled into town. His father found out about the missing casket and kicked Wes out of his house. Wes then went on tour with Screamin' Jay as his stage hand and casket technician, lest Screamin' Jay got locked inside.

King was still preoccupied about the long freeway haul to *Harold & Maude*. He was feeling dizzy.

"I still don't wanna be some half-assed crash test dummy on this mother fuckin' chicken run," King said.

Bishop stopped dead in his tracks.

"Will you relax already. I'm the one that'll be driving. No one knows about your problem."

"It's not a problem," King said. "It's common. You know that famous football player," King misplaced his name. "He has a website, played for the Houston Oilers...Earl Campbell. Earl Campbell, that's his name..."

They kept walking down the tenebrous street when they finally spotted their black hearse. Bishop noticed a black El Camino with tinted windows and gold rims parked behind it. He could smell some primo weed emanating from the El Camino as they approached.

King was still preoccupied about the famous football player that suffered from anxiety like him, so he could feel better about his disorder. Bishop hit the car alarm. It squelched and the back lights flashed red twice.

"Now why would you do that?" King said.

"Do what?"

"The car alarm... nobody's going to steal a hearse."

They were about to load in when they both felt cold steel on their neck. They froze.

"You can have the hearse, take it." King said.

"We don't want the Munster mobile fucka, we want you," Cash said.

Cash, Zip and Wendell forced Bishop and King into the black hearse and climbed in the back. They sat Indian style and kept their guns trained on them.

"Do you know who we is?" Cash said.

Bishop and King were speechless, occasionally staring at each other out of the corner of their eyes. Cash spelled it out for them. "Customers, that's who we is. Regular customers that send you a lot of b'nith."

"Well, we cetainly appieate the bus—"

Cash forced the gun in King's mouth and said, "What was goin' down back there at the Roosevelt?"

"Nothing, just a meeting," Bishop said.

"Meetin' 'bout what?"

"Funeral business stuff."

Cash tossed over a large white scrapbook between Bishop and King. He told them to open it. Bishop reached down and opened up the first page which featured several old Polaroids of dead gangster brothers laid out in their Batesville caskets. Dead victims of drivebys.

"You all charge $8K per brutha," Cash said as he got up real close and personal in Wes Bishop's ear.

"I don't recognize those, ah decedents..." Bishop said. He felt the hard metal of Zip's gun crack the back of his head as he heard the words shouted: SHUT-THE-FUCK-UP-CANDYMAN. Cash was not looking for an answer from Bishop. He went on.

"Listen to me you coupa'la Grim Fairy Tales—" he said. Wendell and Zip liked that one and started laughing like a couple of jackals. Zip lost his grip on the gun and dropped it in the back of the hearse, fishing around for it in the dark.

"Man, what the fuck's wrong wit'chu. Keep yo' gun on him while I'm talkin'," Cash said.

"I can't man, the dude's got Bryllcream or Afro Sheen, or some shit like that all over his head," Zip said. "Made me lose my grip."

Zip wiped his hand on the headrest and curtains of the hearse.

Cash hit him upside the head and then grabbed the scrapbook, forcing it in front of King's face.

"Now take a good, long look," Cash said. "I just got out of the Pen— Pelican Bay. The SHU," he lied, "and I ain't going back in again. And I ain't gonna to wind up in this scrapbook neither, you got that?"

Bishop descried Cash's gold tooth gleaming in the rear-view mirror.

"Look, whatever you want, just take it," King said.

"You damn right we will. We will take whatever the fuck we wants and right now, we are gonna to take a lil' joyride with this here Munster mobile, you got that," Cash said, "and then we might drop by for a cold one later."

Again Zip and Wendall busted a gut laughing at their kingpin's joke. Cash told Bishop and King to get out of the hearse, hand over both of their wallets and any other jewelry— Bishop had as much on as Sammy Davis in his Vegas Stardust days. Cash reminded them that they haven't got all night, to hustle it up. He also demanded Bishop's money clip with $1,000 worth of crisp Ben Franks that he was hiding from King. King shot Bishop a look, pissed off that Bishop was holding out on him. Zip snatched the keys to the hearse.

Cash warned them that they were being watched and not to go to the police or they would end up in his scrapbook.

The g-sters sped off down Hawthorne Avenue and out to LaBrea Boulevard in the black hearse.

The El Camino followed close behind the hearse. Belle Isle was the driver and she laughed her ass off.

Bishop kicked a fence and paced back and forth like a wildcat for several minutes. He finally turned to King and said, "Yeah, right... nobody's going to steal a hearse."

Chapter 11

DEAN WAS THE LAST ONE TO LEAVE
the Hollywood Roosevelt after the prearrangement conference. He stopped at the Tropicana Bar and ordered a
Bloody Mary. He took a seat, alone by the historic David
Hockney pool and observed the Bohemian chic and Gen
Y clicks around the bar and in the poolside cabanas. He
could see the trendy veneers; no one really as tough as ad-
vertised. He wasted some good years in the joint and the
girls were getting younger, he observed, but Dean still had
that cool vibe about him that still caught any eye, at any
place, any time and at any age. Wherever he went, people
thought he was a celebrity . They would stare at him and
try to guess who he was behind the dark Ray-Bans. He
had nothing to prove to anyone. No affectations. No com-
mitments... he just *was* where everyone else wanted to be.
He thought about a Kafka anecdote, where he was alone in
a half-deserted coffee house after midnight when a friend
approached him and asked, "Don't you want to join us?"

Kafka simply replied, "No, I don't."

He started to write a poem on the cocktail napkin before he left; it was something he liked to do on occasion and did it to pass time while he was in jail. Dean finished his Blood Mary. On his way out, he bought a dozen roses from a girl in the lobby. Heads turned when the valet pulled up an exact replica of the Porsche 550 Spyder. He got in, revved it up and pulled out of the lot heading west on Hollywood Boulevard.

He arrived at Barbara Stanwyk's apartment in Westwood —at least that was the cover she used that night — at 10:35 p.m. He parked on Beverly Glen behind a black '49 Mercury. He proceeded up to Apartment #307. When Stanwyck threw open the door, the tears gushed like Niagara. She was a real number. An anachronistic plaything from Hollywood's Golden Age.

"My condolences," Dean said.

He handed her the dozen roses, shooting a quick glance at the 50's style decorum; vintage posters and framed lobby cards of: *Sorry Wrong Number, Double Indemnity, The Bride Walks Out*. She handed him a scotch and refreshed the rocks.

"He was such a good man," she said. "He had so much going for him."

"He would've wanted you to move on," Dean said.

"How could I?" she said, "He's never coming back... gone for good."

He gently handed her the card from the roses and

said, "Death is never final for people like us."

He pulled up her chin and brought her lips to his, wiped her cheeks and then seemed to embrace her for an eternity.

Stanwyck finally released Dean's grip and led him into the bedroom.

Chapter 12

MAPLE LEFT THE W HOTEL BEFORE 9 A.M.
He figured he could walk down to Westwood Memorial
and be the first one on-site as they opened the gates for
another day of business. He grabbed his coffee to go, his
foldout tourist map of the cemetery grounds, and Stan
Glen's urn in the Payless shoe box. On the way over, he
managed to pluck a flower from a nearby apartment on
Glendon. As he arrived, the groundskeeper was just swing-
ing the first gate open.

"Good morning," Maple said. "Where can I find Natalie Wood?"

The groundskeeper pointed in an eastern direction and
spoke in broken English.

"Gracias," Maple said.

Maple felt that he was being watched, so he snapped a
few photos of the cemetery and placed a flower on Natalie's
grave. He then knelt down and dipped his hand in a terra
cotta potter at the base of the headstone. He fished

around the soil until he located the mailbox key that Bishop had left behind. Maple made it a point to chat with the groundskeeper on his way out. He asked him if he knew anything about the night Natalie Wood drowned off the coast of Catalina Island. The groundskeeper only understood a third of what Maple was saying and just kept nodding and politely saying "sí." The groundskeeper studied him while he was talking and then Maple excused himself and made it a point to tell him he was off to Catalina Island, but failed to notice the silver *Big Sleep* hearse parked in Westwood Memorial's circular drive.

Coffin Joe was alone, without any tourists. He tipped his chauffeurs cap to conceal his face and proceeded to shadow Maple on his way out. Maple then hiked up to the local Mail Boxes Etc.. and opened the oversized box, #130. He placed the Payless shoe box inside and removed a large envelope. He stuffed it in his cheap Members Only windbreaker and called for a cab.

Maple arrived at the Long Beach port at the Downtown Catalina Landing. It was located in the heart of LBC along the waterfront beside the Pike and the Aquarium of the Pacific. When Maple arrived he purchased one ticket for the Catalina Express, departure time 12:15 p.m. to Avalon.

He downed several double martinis at the Catalina Lounge but never boarded the boat. He spent a great deal of time talking to the bartender about what happened to Natalie Wood that night on The Splendor. Maple was certain that the skipper knew the real story. The bartender was not familiar with Natalie Wood. He was too young.

Maple talked about *Westside Story,* but the bartender was more interested in the Lakers on TV.

Maple was unaware that Gladwin had put a tail on him. After Maple snuck out into an incoming crowd, Agent Kim interviewed the bartender and confirmed that Mike Maple was rattling on about some actress; he thought it was Natalie Portman. Agent Kim then made a subsequent call to Gladwin and agreed to meet at Mary & Rob's diner in Westwood.

Coffin Joe observed Agent Kim from the small food court. He pretended to be interested in the helicopter flight brochure, while he sipped a Snapple with a straw through his bushy mustache. After Agent Kim left, he tossed the brochure in a trash can and walked out.

Chapter 13

GLADWIN SAT IN THE BACK BOOTH
of the restaurant studying the menu when Agent Kim strolled in, grinning ear to ear. He slid into the circular booth, placing a backpack at his feet.

"What's up, G-Man," Agent Kim said.

"I don't fucking get it." Gladwin said. "James DeRossa pops into town under the alias of James Dean and the TSA or our goddamn Homeland Security doesn't bat an eyelash... just passes him right through."

Agent Kim grabbed the menu, perused the greasiest item on it and tossed it back in front of Gladwin, who was looking around for the waitress.

"He's not a terrorist," Agent Kim said.

"It doesn't matter. He's an ex-con."

Gladwin opened a folder with a photocopied airline ticket that showed passenger: James Dean. Kim glanced at it superficially, then laughed.

"Generation gap, G-Man."

"Generation gap, my ass," Gladwin said, "try indolence. I'm sure the TSA scrutinized his under 3.0 ounce liquids... pisses me off."

"Pisses me off too. You know, the last time I went to Vegas they took my shaving cream, shampoo and Listerine— I had to re-buy all that crap again when I got to my hotel."

Gladwin decided to go with the heart-smart choice on the menu: The salad.

"Is our server ever coming back? I'm starving," Agent Kim said.

"I sent her back to the kitchen to find out what type of oil the chicken is cooked in. "Screw it, I'll stop at Trader Joe's and buy something organic on the way home."

"Not me, I'm getting the Patti-Melt smothered in grease, onions and cheese," Agent Kim said as he handed Gladwin back the photocopy of the airline ticket. "Still, DeRossa did serve his time." He reached under the table and unzipped the bag.

"He's setting up a heist," Gladwin said. "Our man on the inside said *Harold & Maude* is in motion."

"His father taught him how to set up a procession, I'll give 'em that."

Gladwin was becoming more irratated by Agent Kim's complacence.

Agent Kim pulled out the Payless shoe box and boldly placed it right in the middle of the table next to the condiments.

"What the hell is that?" Gladwin said. The question was rhetorical. Gladwin's mind flashed back to Mike Maple with the Payless shoe box. The real question was how in the hell did Agent Kim get his hands on it so fast.

"I sure do love the Patriot Act, G-Man."

Gladwin opened it up and carefully pulled out the gold urn. Agent Kim sat in suspense, ogling him to go on and open it. At this point their server was back, frozen in her footsteps, repulsed at the sight of the urn on top of the table. Gladwin told the waitress they would need a few more minutes to decide.

He slowly opened the lid and peeked inside.

There were no ashes.

There was certainly no Stan Glen.

There was however, cigarette butts galore; The urn was nothing more then an expensive ashtray and clever parlor trick that Maple brought into town. Distractive trash.

"Well...?" Agent Kim said.

Gladwin was still speechless. Slackjawed. He was expecting Stan Glen or some other interesting artifact, perhaps a clue to OGR or OCN. Gladwin's face was beet red when he finally cleared his throat and said, "Maple just dug himself a deeper grave."

MICHAEL P. NAUGHTON

Chapter 14

"*ANGELO'S ASHES: TRUTH IS STRANGER THAN FICTION*," read the January 2005 AP article that Gladwin pulled from his stack of yellowed newspaper clippings on his desk. The case made national headlines when the New Jersey police investigated the Tri-State Crematory and unearthed, well let's just say, every family's nightmare; thanks to a dog who brought home a human skull for its owner. Angelo Antonini, who took over his father's crematorium, told authorities that his incinerator was broken. They found bodies everywhere: in the garage, in the nearby lake—55 had been positively identified — at least 9 came from local New Jersey funeral homes. Officials from Fairfield Township and the New Jersey Bureau of Investigation said there were over 130 bodies stashed there. Families were told to bring in their loved ones' remains to the makeshift site, Fairfield County Civic Center, to verify authenticity. What they found was nothing more than potting soil and cement dust. Local funeral directors said the undertaker "seemed" to be an honest businessman. The word "seemed" in articles always irked Gladwin. Why not just say: I did business with the bastard and had no idea he was a sick bastard and was burying poor bastards in his backyard, like family pets, and pocketing the cash. But the Jersey community knew their local undertaker as an upstanding citizen. A real staple of the community. Gladwin laughed to himself, so was John Wayne Gacy.

Gladwin had seen his fair share of these types of grim stories with reputable establishments. Fraud, embezzlement, multiple burials and profits of death— Even Catholic archdioceses made deals with the big conglomerates in order not to lose their market shares of burials— Gladwin wanted to take a *Dirty Harry* approach to dealing with these bastards and had zero tolerance for bureaucracy. He smiled at the 8 x 10 signed, glossy photo of Clint Eastwood on his desk. He shifted his gaze to the Payless shoe box that sat next to it. Incensed. He plucked out a brochure that was underneath the box entitled: *Paying Final Respects: Your Rights When Buying Funeral Goods And Services.* He reflected on the evolution of the FTC's Funeral Rule. The rule was implemented in 1984 and established the following:

- *The Consumer's Right to Choose;*
- *Prices must be quoted over the phone;*
- *Undertakers would be prohibited from misstating a law— specifically with reference to embalming (embalming is not required by law);*
- *The cheapest casket must be displayed with the*

others.

• *Funeral providers would be prohibited from telling the customer that the "eternal sealer" casket will preserve the corpse for a long or indefinite time.*

Gladwin had experience with this back in the 80's while investigating funeral fraud. He worked with the Attorney General and had friends that were lawyers for the FTC. But studies had shown that over 10 years later, in 1994, compliance was at an all time low. Funeral homes routinely neglected to give consumers a GPL (General Price List) as required by the FTC. So in 1996, in order to twist a few arms, they cracked down with the help of the National Funeral Directors Association (NFDA), who submitted a proposal to the Commission for an industry self-regulatory program called F.R.O.P. or Funeral Rule Offenders Program. The purpose of F.R.O.P. is to keep the offenders out of court and eliminate endless litigation. Otherwise, if they faced law enforcement action by the FTC it could result in civil penalties of as much as $11,000 per violation. Violators that opted for F.R.O.P. could make voluntary payments to the U.S. Treasury instead. By 2006, the FTC made undercover visits to 100 funeral homes in seven states to assess their compliance with the Funeral Rule.

This time around compliance had improved. Only 12 violators were found and had to face the prospect of FTC lawsuits that could lead to a court order and civil penalties. These homes elected to participate in F.R.O.P. Gladwin pulled the press release from the FTC.

It read:

1,850 homes in 33 states had been swept and completed by 2006.

All this was peanuts compared to the buried money from *Operation Grim Reaper*, Gladwin's real passion.

There was a link in there somewhere.

There had to be.

Detective Mike Maple shows up at the same time as James DeRossa, aka "James Dean." Ostensibly he flew in to offer assistance with OGR, yet he doesn't offer shit. He deliberately lies and concocts some sentimental fish story about Stan Glen's ashes; the urn turns out to be an ashtray.

Gladwin turned on the TASCAM recorder again and replayed the conversation inside DeRossa & Sons Mortuary.

"Cash at the Y." Stop. Rewind. Replay.

For a long period of time, Gladwin sat bewildered by the file box that Maple left behind. He finally started rifling through the contents. He took out his old tape reels and carefully replaced them with Maples OGR tapes.

Agent Kim knocked on the door and informed Gladwin that they traced the two dummy caskets ordered from Coffin Depot to a Nicholas Ray in Detroit. Agent Kim was certain that Nicholas Ray was actually Ray Driscol, aka "Quincy." The Smothers Brothers had become persons of interest when their mortuary in West Hollywood mysteriously burnt down two years ago. Arson was always suspected but nothing would stick. They maintained, to insurance investigators, that one of their competitors took a match to it. With the insurance payout they opened Coffin Depot, LLC and ran the business out of a U-Store -It storage unit in West Hollywood. Prior to the arson incident, they had been in violation and were currently enrolled as participants in F.R.O.P. and most recently re-enrolled for an unrelated charge at Coffin Depot. Gladwin started investigating Coffin Depot and other wholesalers like Coffins "R" Us when the FTC started receiving complaints of boycotts; casket factories refusing to sell to wholesale casket companies like Coffin Depot.

The Smothers Brothers had become the eBay of the casket business— they even had a storefront on eBay.

The problem was, often when customers purchased a discounted coffin from the Smothers Brothers, it would mysteriously arrive busted up at the funeral home. The mortician on the receiving end would have no explanation, but then the unctuous undertaker would upsell a pricey Batesville to the grieving family in the interest of time.

Gladwin got wiretaps and found local mortuaries were also placing threatening phone calls to these wholesalers in the middle of the night instructing them to "have coffins ready for themselves." Gladwin thought the whole funeral business was a racket and signed up with a local not-for-profit memorial society called: *Down To Earth Memorial Society of Los Angeles.* For a nominal fee, he could have a dignified send off at a wholesale price and not have his fellow detectives visit him "laid out" in some morbid tradition perpetuated by corporate avarice.

He switched on the old reel-to-reel tape recorder once

again. Tape recording CAN-10OCT74-FRANK DER-OSSA. Time is approximately 9:45 P.M.

Detective: There was a heist tonight at Windsor Raceway... someone pulled a big job...

Frank DeRossa: Is that why my horse didn't pay off?

Detective: What were you doing in Canada this evening?

Frank DeRossa: Convention. A little gambling afterwards. It's legal.

Detective: What kind of convention?

Frank DeRossa: NFDA. It's for undertakers...That stands for...

Detective: ...we know what it stands for...(long pause) Have you had any recent affiliation or sit downs with the Caruana-Cuntrera Clan?

Frank DeRossa: Can't say I have.

Detective: How 'bout Vito Rizzuto?

Frank DeRossa: Should I?

Detective: They are the Canadian Mafia. The U.S. Department of Justice and the FBI have been aware of their drug trafficking, money laundering and now they have their greasy hands in several businesses... they know bankers and lawyers that can wash money from here to Nova Scotia. We're seeing a lot of it pass through Montreal.

Frank DeRossa: Like I said, I run a funeral business.

Detective: Does your wife know you're over here?

Frank DeRossa: Sure.

Detective: Does she know you're over here with someone else's wife?

Frank DeRossa: You referrin' to Josephine Franzetta?

Detective: Yeah.

Frank DeRossa: She's just some broad that works at the track.

Detective: Some broad that wasn't working tonight.

Frank DeRossa: She wasn't with me.

Detective: We know that. Any idea where she disappeared to?

Frank DeRossa: No. (long pause) So when do I get my two white hearses back?

Detective: We'll let you know when they come off the assembly line, okay? (laughter in the background by other Royal Canadian Mounted Police or RCMP)

RCMP: We have two Russians and two black hearses in custody on the Canadian side of the Ambassador Bridge. They were headed back from Detroit.

Frank DeRossa: I don't make the connection.

RCMP: A shipment of diamonds from South Africa was passing through customs... they were intercepted and never passed through.

Frank DeRossa: I don't know any Russian undertakers and don't know who hit Windsor racetrack.

Detective: What was your big hurry back this evening?

Frank DeRossa: I was on my way to Greektown.

Detective: You laid out some big dough on the Trifecta and then just left without seeing your horse come in.

Frank DeRossa: I've got a business to run.

RCMP: The Russians claim they were coming back from Greektown.

Frank DeRossa: (laughs)

Detective: Earlier you said, "is that why my horse didn't

come in. How did you know he didn't come in if you left?"

The tape ended there.

Gladwin took out the black and white RCMP photos from the siege at the Windsor Tunnel and studied them closely. There was a photo of Big Frank DeRossa leaning against his white hearse smoking a cigarette and extending a pack of Dorals to a customs agent. Frank DeRossa sounded tough and cool, like Robert Mitchum, on the tapes. He had a great voice.

There was a photo of the Windsor tunnel traffic backing up. The tunnel pipeline between the U.S. and Canada is the only subaqueous tunnel in the world. Gladwin was claustrophobic. The thought of being in tunnel gridlock made his palms sweat. He tossed the photo aside and pulled out another photo of the Ambassador Bridge and the two black hearses. There were also numerous photos of the black and white hearses being inspected, with the RCMP standing by so regal; examining the paperwork, checking under the hearse hoods, and opening caskets.

Gladwin laughed and blurted out loud, "Dudley Do-Rights."

He stared back out over Wilshire Boulevard. It was getting late. He turned back towards the tape deck and replaced the reels with the previous reels he was listening to. He took additional notes and then placed a phone call to his paid informant. They agreed to meet at Griffith Park Observatory near the bust of the real, legendary James Dean.

Chapter **15**

DEAN SAT ON THE EDGE OF THE BED,
half-awake and half-dressed on the satin sheets. He stood
up and stretched in front of the full length mirror; an expensive antique from Melrose. He tilted his right shoulder
forward to get a better look at the cat scratches on his
back. Stanwyck started to rustle. She sat up. Her blonde
locks flopped over one eye. Her other eye smeared with
black mascara— man, she really looked the part. Dean
made his way for the rest of his clothes, smirking.

"Easy on the Stanwyck next time, aye."

"You said you wanted me to drive you crazy."

"I did," Dean said, "just not *Dragonwyck* crazy."

They both laughed at his bad joke. Stanwyck anxiously
opened the condolence card Dean had given her the night
before, a few crisp c-notes edging out. Her eyes lit up at
the sight of them.

"Wowza." she said.

"Do you have any coffee around this joint?" He asked.

"I figured," Stanwyck said, "since you got your hambone boiled, now we can get to know each other a little better. I'm a rental... there are no late fees and there's this cool Starbucks up the street."

Dean checked his Blackberry. Quincy texted him. He scrolled the message:

Egyptian Theater.
7 p.m. The Enforcer.
Humphrey Bogart.

He holstered his Blackberry on his hip and said, "Sorry sweetheart, Daddy-o's got to go. Gotta date with Bogie at the Egyptian."

Dean picked up a *Hollywood Reporter* from the nightstand and said, "So how is the acting coming?"

Stanwyck hated those earth shattering kind of Q and As.

"I had a casting director tell me to lose the grandmother garb and get real the other day," she said. "Can you believe that? They have no respect for old Hollywood."

Dean grabbed his keys, half-listening.

"I'll bet Garbo is turning in her grave over today's young Hollywood."

Dean bent over the bed and kissed her goodbye and said, "Thanks for the roll in the hay."

She did one of the worst impersonations of Lauren Bacall he had ever heard and said in an overly dramatic tone, "You know how to whistle, don't you?"

Dean didn't respond.

He walked out the door on that note.

Chapter **16**

DETECTIVE GLADWIN WAITED IN FRONT OF the James Dean bust at the Griffith Observatory. He watched the shuttles and the cars coming and going, winding up the road, dropping off tourists and picking them up. Business was good since the new renovation. Joe Smothers startled him when he tapped him on the back.

"Jumpy," Joe said.

"You're late," Gladwin said as he pulled out an envelope from his jacket.

Joe glanced inside and smiled at the contents. It was stuffed with $3,000 cash. Joe placed the envelope in his suit jacket and lit up a fat cigar. He looked around the grounds, amazed.

Gladwin fanned the smoke from his face.

"What do you think of the renovation?" Joe said.

"They moved Dean's bust," Gladwin said. "Watch with the smoke."

Joe turned away from Gladwin, expelling smoke as he

examined the bust, and then noticed the Hollywood sign in the background.

"I guess they did, didn't they."

Tourists began to flock around them. An Asian tourist asked Gladwin to take his photo in front of the bust. Gladwin snapped off a few digital photos and quickly moved away from the tourists, keeping a low profile.

"Everything's a go with *Harold & Maude,*" Joe said.

"You're not being paid to tell me what I already know," Gladwin said as he stopped in his tracks. "Tell me something I don't know."

Joe handed Gladwin the envelope that Dean had distributed at the prearrangement conference. Gladwin carefully inspected the documents.

"The question is *where* is *Harold & Maude?*" Gladwin said.

"If I knew that, would I be standing here talking to you?"

Gladwin knew never to trust paid informants and he was always quick to remind them.

"Look asshole, talking to me is what keeps a piece of shit like you from doing time on the inside. You get me DeRossa, and you remain free. You fuck up and sell me some disinformation, and I'll close the coffin lid on you too. You're a two-bit snitch, and don't forget it." Gladwin fixated on the map and said, "I see that the disinterment is happening at Ascension in Orange County, but where are the crypts?"

"He wouldn't tell us that," Joe said, as he watched the same purple hearse from Hollywood Forever pull up and park behind a yellow cab. He wondered if they were working with Gladwin. "He told us we would get further instructions when we got there... from some superintendent on duty."

There were a few minutes of uncomfortable silence as Gladwin authenticated the envelope contents. Joe finally broke the silence and said, "What about Vic?"

"What about him," Gladwin said, reading.

"He walks too when this is all through, right?"

Gladwin stopped reading and glared at Joe Smothers, smirking at the thought of what he was about to say next.

"No, no, that's not the deal we made, and that's not the way it works. One of you goes in, the other remains on the outside... a free man; which one that is I really don't give two shits about. You deal with that on your own, pal. It's not my problem or the department's problem."

Joe began to raise his voice, arousing some of the tourists.

"You're asking me to sell out my own brother,"

"You don't have much of a choice," Gladwin said. "Actually you do: you or him." He reminded him to keep his voice down.

"He's trying to turn his life around," Joe said.

"He can do that in prison."

"He's innocent in all this. He doesn't even know I'm working with you."

"He's committing a crime. He is a co-conspirator. Innocent, my ass."

"We're helping you nail DeRossa."

"It's not an even trade— when we take down a whole

ring... let's just say there are sacrifices," Gladwin said. "I mean, what is it with you guys anyway? It's always the same old song and dance. You're out to save your own ass, but when it comes time to pay the piper you have a change of heart, when none of this shit would be happening in the first place if you were a straight up, law-abiding citizen. You chose to be Public Enemy #1 not John Q Public. No deal."

Joe was a rat. A king sized, Henry Hill of a rat. But he was caged and Gladwin had him behind the eight ball. He took a long drag from his cigar and blew the smoke into Gladwin's face.

"Didn't I tell you not to do that."

"Do what," Joe said.

"The smoke, that's what," Gladwin said. "My wife died from second hand smoke. Never smoked a day in her life and was diagnosed with lung cancer. Just died like that. I went through hell with her through that ordeal. Watching her wither away to nothing... I've got a big piece of granite with my name on it next to her, waiting. Just waiting back in Indiana for that other date between the hyphen— Paid a small fortune for that plot so that we could be buried side by side. Still paying on the damn thing. Some undertaker SOB upsold me in my hour of grief, and I found out later that I paid three times what it was actually worth. So please, keep the goddamn second hand smoke out of my face."

Joe was speechless and half-listening, still troubled about selling his brother out for his own freedom. They walked towards the direction of Gladwin's car. It was a tan

'03 Sedan.

"Where is the transfer taking place?" Gladwin asked.

Joe hesitated a moment knowing he had nothing to lose.

"There isn't one. Those two black dudes I told you about—

"—Bishop & King?"

"Right, Bishop and King," Joe said. "Those two are taking *Harold & Maude* right to the Anaheim Convention Center during the trade show."

Gladwin pulled out the two tickets to the Death Expo. He stared Joe down for a few moments then asked, "You wouldn't be lying to me, would you?"

Joe thought about it for a moment, smiled and said, "Did Sean Connery polish coffins as a kid."

"I don't know, did he?"

"He did... at least that's what Dean said."

"I wouldn't believe anything that guy said."

Gladwin got in the Sedan and gave Joe back all of the envelope's contents. He reached behind the seat and pulled out a sunflower from the bouquet he picked up earlier from Hollywood Forever. He looked around and smiled, a sinister smile.

"It's a good day to be above ground, Joey." He gave the sunflower to Joe and drove off.

Joe Smothers watched the tan Sedan head back down the hill.

Chapter **17**

WES BISHOP WONDERED WHY THE CHAPEL smelled like catfish. He had been gone for several hours with no accountability and returned with a Target shopping bag. He found King, business as usual, working on Ms. Barbara Clark, a decedent, for the next day's viewing. The smell was emanating from a George Foreman Grill in the corner by the casket.

Bishop also noticed the red and white checkered lining that King had placed inside the Batesville casket to resemble a picnic basket; a picnic basket casket.

"Good lord, why does the chapel smell like catfish," Bishop said.

"'Cause Ms. Clark ordered it," King said. "Did you pick up the deck of playing cards like I asked you to?"

Bishop didn't answer. He did move in closer to examine King's face, just to make sure he was feeling okay. He glanced back at Ms. Clark who was stiff as a board.

"Ms. Clark is dead," he said, "why would she be ordering catfish? Have you lost your marbles?"

King tore off his rubber apron and threw it aside, incensed. "Her family ordered it," King said. "No, I'm not okay. You did forget to pick up the playing cards and tablecloth like I asked you to, didn't you?"

King rummaged through the Target bag and found toilet paper, toothpaste, dog food and Gatorade, but no tablecloth or playing cards. "I see you didn't forget to pick up food for that damn dog."

"Don't start in on poor 'ole Rudolph again. That dog is good protection. If we'd had 'em with us, those brothers would've been Foster Farms or KFC the minute they sat their baggy, gangsta asses in our hearse."

"Don't start in...? Let's just say... I have good reason," King said with a penatrating glare.

Bishop crouched down near Rudolph, pulled out a knockoff gold cigarette case and lit up a smoke. He inhaled, taking intermittent swigs of Gatorade from the Target bag. "The other thing is," Bishop said, "I also had to check into renting a hearse 'cuz remember, ours got jacked, and I just can't fucking call up Avis-Rent-A Car and order one."

Bishop watched King open up one end of the picnic basket on the table and strategically place some fruit on the top, arranging it in a pyramid shape, then standing back and keenly observing it with a shrewd, aesthetic eye.

"Don, what the hell is wrong with you?" Bishop said looking around the chapel. "This is a funeral home not a Bridge Club or County Fair. Talk about high-falutin."

King went over to the George Foreman Grill and flipped the catfish. Rudolph their Red Nose Pit Bull was positioned underneath the grill waiting for a piece to fall from the sky. King hated the dog after a mortifying incident during a funeral, and ever since the incident he would just say he had "good reason" and then Bishop would ask him not to get into those "reasons" and that was the end of that discussion.

Rudolph was actually Bishop's Pit Bull— he rescued the Pit from an animal shelter that later turned out to be breeding Pits for fighting. As a rule, they always kept Rudolph locked up during funerals because, quite frankly, he scared the shit out of anyone who encountered him. The door had to be dead-bolted shut because Rudolph was strong as a bull and would ram his head into the door like *Jaws* against Captain Quint's boat.

Normally no one ever heard a peep out of Rudolph, but on that day he was restless. Pent up. The decedent, Alexis Macomb, was 92 years old and died of natural causes. The irony was, she was terrified of dogs her whole natural life. She was a cat person; owned 12 of them in her later years. Her kids used to complain of the cat urine smell and she would say, "You can't smell nothin' with *Tidy Cat.*" Everything was feline themed decorum in her house. Cat china, kitty-cat oven mitts and dish towels, and now she was resting peacefully in her kitty-cat apron and slippers. The funeral was going well for the Macomb family that day. About 80 attendees. People even thanked Bishop and King for the beautiful service and complimented them, on their way out, on just how stunning Grandma Macomb looked.

Each of the mourners walked up to the front of the

parlor and paid their final respects to Grandma Macomb. However, disruption started when intense scratching sounds were coming from the door behind Bishop and King in the back of the parlor.

Attendees turned their head toward the back of the room. Bishop and King nodded to them uncomfortably, hands clasped in front of them in that cordial undertaker pose. King would kick the door with his heel and then Rudolph would stop for a few minutes... but then the scratching and digging of claws would then persist again.

There was more sobbing from mourners.

More somber organ.

More scratching and digging, and then more disdainful, dirty looks directed at Bishop and King.

They were about through with the last of the mourners when the scratching became more intense. In hindsight— perhaps Rudolph knew that Grandma Macomb was such a cat lover too.

There was more sobbing. More scratching. More snorting. Then a loud yelp. Bishop put his ear to the door, concerned.

He cupped his ear with his hand and listened at various levels on the door like a skilled heart surgeon seeking a beat.

He heard nothing.

No scratching.

Nothing. Silence.

He slowly unlocked the door. That was a mistake.

The door creaked. Followed by more sobbing.

The next thing that happened was unimaginable.

DEATHRYDE: REBEL WITHOUT A CORPSE

The door swung wide open and Rudolph the Red Nose Pit Bull charged the casket and Ms. Macomb like a locomotive.

Hysterical women were shrieking all at once at the top of their lungs. Mourners dove in all directions. Folding chairs flew in the air.

Rudolph went straight for Ms. Macomb's neck and clamped on, knocking the casket over and rolling the body onto the floor. The Pit Bull's jaws were locked.

More hysterical screaming ensued.

"Oh my God, it's got grandma," someone shouted. "Do something."

"Kill it with somethin'," someone else screamed.

"Shoot the muthafucker," another mourner shouted.

Five courageous men finally jumped over the casket and attempted to pry the jaws open. Five big guys tackled that bitch of a Pit Bull like they were playing for the Raiders. King finally grabbed a nearby glass terrarium arrangement and smashed it over Rudolph's head.

The jaws... popped open.

The final damages exceeded $50,000 in an out-of-court settlement. The Better Business Bureau, along with the NFDA, investigated Bishop and King, but Rudolph was spared doggy heaven after it was deemed an unfortunate accident and not gross negligence.

Yes... King certainly had "good reason."

"You're the reason we've never made a dime in this business," King said.

"Really?" Bishop said and then went in for the kill. "I 've got two words for you: Colonial Pen."

It was true, Don King was responsible for his own mal-feasance when he was busted posing as Lou Rawls from Colonial Pen Life Insurance— he did do a spot-on Lou Rawls inpersonation over the phone and people on the other end just hypnotically wrote checks... until the real Lou Rawl's attorneys caught wind of the scam.

"You'll Never Find Another Love Like Mine," promised Rawl's attorney. They hunted him down and served him with an arrest warrant. King served two years in jail. He also had to participate in the Funeral Rules Offenders Program after his release, an incident that King tended to downplay in discussions.

They were both up to their necks in debt and *Harold & Maude* was their only ticket out.

King said, "I have straightened my act up since then." He looked away and began fiddling with some *Town & Country* magazines by the casket. He picked up the lat-est copy of *Mortuary Management* magazine and jabbed it into Bishop's face. "Here, read this month's issue about the mortician in Westchester that's pullin' down six-figures in personalized send offs. It's the newest, hottest trend. This guy is makin' a killing on this right here while we're wast-ing our time with this half-assed heist. Shit, we might as well invite OJ."

"Leave his ass outta this," Bishop said. "So, how much did all this extra shit cost you?"

"It's nominal, Wes," King said, "compared to the return on investment and repeat business after word gets around that we... I mean, I know how to throw a funeral."

"Don, you won't hafta' worry about this shit after tomorrow."

King turned around and jabbed the spatula in Bishop's face.

"We're still runnin' a business here," he said, "and we've got obligations... legal obligations to fulfill. Ms. Clark's family paid us in full. We have a contract. I ain't going to go back into that Funeral Rule Offenders Program again and I'll tell you another thing, when the detectives come sniffing around here, the only thing they're gonna smell is catfish."

"You've flipped your lid," Bishop said. "The only thing the police are going to arrest you for is having a cookout with a corpse."

Chapter **18**

"SOMETIMES DEATH IS JUST A COIN TOSS,"
Coffin Joe said. It was the day before *Harold & Maude* and
he was giving his tourists their money's worth of celebrity
death trivia.

The Big Sleep hearse had just left Westwood Memorial
Mortuary and was now heading south on Beverly Glen towards Santa Monica Boulevard and Hollywood Forever.

"Carol Lombard, who was married to Clark Gable, could not make up her mind" he said, "whether to take a
plane or a train in 1942. So she tossed a coin and opted for
the plane."

One of the tourists with a thick Jersey accent rudely interrupted the story with the question of whether the head
or tail of the coin corresponded with the plane or train.
Coffin Joe couldn't remember, so he went with tails for the
plane to move the story along.

"Needless to say the coin toss cost her her life and she per-
ished in the plane crash at just 33 years old. A coin toss also
killed Ritchie Valens when he persuaded this cat named
Tommy Allsup—"

DEATHRYDE: REBEL WITHOUT A CORPSE

The Jersey tourist interrupted Coffin Joe again, needing to know which, heads or tails, corresponded with the plane or the train. Coffin Joe was getting annoyed and informed him that there was not a train this time. It was a bus and the plane was unequivocally "heads."

The tourist, being a wise guy, tested the universe's logic and Coffin Joe and said: "Well then, a side of a coin does not determine your fate, it's just bad luck. Lombard chose tails and Valens chose heads."

Coffin Joe suggested he go read *Rosencrantz and Guildenstern* or rent the movie from Netflix when he goes back home, and moved on to the next story as he approached the intersection of Beverly Glen and Santa Monica Boulevard.

"Famous crash site here folks," he said. "Ernie Kovacs was visiting the great Billy Wilder one night on January 23rd, 1962, when he crashed his car— incidentally, if you ever get a chance, rent *Some Like It Hot*. The gangster bootleggers posing as undertakers were such a hoot—"

"Yeah, like gangster undertakers would really be credible in today's times," the Jersey smartass from the back of the hearse said.

Coffin Joe thought about the *Harold & Maude* heist and hoped the Feds thought like this joker. He grinned.

"Anyway, they found Ernie Kovacs dead with his Cuban cigar..."

Coffin Joe caught a glimpse of Dean's silver Spyder Porshe zooming by in the opposite direction on Beverly Glen. When they got to Hollywood Forever, Coffin Joe unloaded his tourists from the side of the silver hearse.

He leaned against the hearse and pulled a coin out of his pocket. He shouted back at the smartass tourist who was headed towards the gift shop.

He wished him a safe trip back home while he was tossing the quarter in the air, then he tossed the coin to the tourist. The tourist caught the quarter and grimaced, laughing uncomfortably. He kept looking back over his shoulder at Coffin Joe, but never once looked at the quarter.

Another Big Sleep silver hearse pulled up behind Coffin Joe to relieve him for the next shift.

Chapter 19

BARBARA STANWYCK STOOD IN LINE at Starbucks waiting for her Frappuccino. Her nose was buried in today's *Hollywood Reporter*. She sported her dark, retro shades, fantasizing about getting mobbed by fans. Billie Holiday's *Good Morning Heartache* played throughout the coffee shop. They called her drink, she grabbed her Frappuccino and took a seat in the back of the shop. Detective Gladwin was waiting for her.

"Double-crossing dame," Gladwin said.

She cracked a smile as she wiped the lipstick from the plastic lid.

He passed her a Grande coffee cup across the table. She peeked under the lid and took note of the curled wad of Ben Franks. Stanwyck said, "Now that's what I call a Grande— Would you like some of my coffee?"

Gladwin smiled and said, "I don't drink coffee, just green tea. So where is James Dean headed?"

"Eqyptian Theatre in Hollywood."

He got up, looked around Starbucks furtively and said, "I'll let you know when the next audition is. You did good kiddo... real good."

She opened up her *Hollywood Reporter* and began the morning ritual of circling productions and sending out headshots. She was alone. Still an unknown. On the fringe.

She called out to Gladwin, "Hey, you don't happen to know any real agents do you?"

He stopped for a moment and thought about that loaded question and proceeded out the door. He checked his notepad for the next address on his long list of suspects.

Chapter **20**

GLADWIN STOOD LOOKING AT HIS REFLECTION
in the cooler of sunflowers at Daisy Acres Floral Creations
shop. He was startled by a friendly "hello" from behind
the counter. He turned to an attractive woman in her mid-
sixties. This was Daisy Acres, owner and full time floral
arranger.

"Can I help you, sir?"

"You're Daisy Acres?" Gladwin said as he handed her his
business card. The plain white card simply read:

Detective Hank Hellion Gladwin
F-B-I, Special Agent

"Is this about the credit card fraud, Mr. Gladwin?" Daisy seemed amused, almost toying with him.

"I wish it were that simple," Gladwin said. "Do you recall any recent arrangements being delivered to Westwood
Memorial?

"No, but that doesn't mean anything," Daisy said. "I

suppose I can check with my driver."

Gladwin had noticed her looking at the sunflowers in the cooler while she was thinking.

Gladwin said, "Is your driver here?"

"No, I'm afraid not. He's gone for the day... slacker." She laughed.

"Then I would assume you keep a logbook of some sort?"

"Of course."

He followed her around to the counter and watched her rummage through brown paper, stems, vases, and underneath stacks of newspapers.
She stopped for a moment and then looked up at Gladwin. An epiphany.

"Yes, I do remember that day," she said. "He took an extra lunch... said he had an audition... Actors! It was Monday."

"Perhaps you could give him a call," Gladwin said, "and jar his memory."

Daisy picked up the phone and started dialing, then slammed down the phone, startling Gladwin.

"Nicolas Ray," she shouted.

You mean Ray Driscol, aka "Quincy," Gladwin thought to himself.

"Yes," she said, "Nicolas Ray was the man who ordered the arrangements. He was calling from Michigan. Claimed he was a fan of Monroe, Martin and..." She seemed to be having a senior moment, so Gladwin filled in the blanks.

"Bugsy Siegel?"

"Yes, Bugsy Siegel."

She continued on, "Yes, that was the third one, but he, of course, is buried at Hollywood Forever. So two arrangements went to Westwood Memorial and one went to Hollywood Forever."

She glanced back at the cooler and at the sunflowers.

"Sunflowers. All three bouquets. Just like the ones over there that you were staring at when you came in, Detective Gladwin."

Gladwin paused for a moment and started to browse nearby items. His eyes stopped on a crystal unicorn. He picked it up and examined it.

"You see, Detective Gladwin," she said, "when you came in, I thought you were investigating the credit card fraud."

"Credit card fraud?" Gladwin said, but didn't follow.

"Yes," Daisy said. "A few weeks ago we hired a part-time gal from Orange County. She was only here a week or so, claimed to be taking classes at UCLA. She complained about her student loans and boyfriend and broken family, you name it. Anyway, I got several customer complaints about suspicious charges and then requests for charge-backs on credit cards, and well... I thought you were—"

"I wish it were that simple, Ms. Acres." Gladwin said as he smiled. He seemed fond of the crystal unicorn. He flipped it over and looked at the gold 'Made In China' label on the bottom.

Gladwin looked up, troubled.

"I'd like to buy this for my sister," Gladwin said as he dug out a few crumpled $20 bills from his pants. He handed the money and the unicorn over the counter, keeping an eye on the logbook resting next to the roll of brown paper.

"Could you wrap that," he said, "if you don't mind."

"No, no trouble at all," Daisy said as she pulled a sheet of paper from underneath a stack.

Gladwin's mind was racing. He glanced at the ribbons behind her and asked if she would mind putting a bow on it. Daisy Acres turned her back on him for a moment and Gladwin swiped the logbook.

"Is your sister okay?"

"She's recovering from back surgery," Gladwin said.

"Poor thing."

"She'll be fine. Been dealing with it her whole life."

"Where does she live?"

"Oh, she's back in Detroit."

Daisy was quiet for a few minutes, perfecting the creases in the gift wrap and carefully taping the sides. A real perfectionist.

"I have to catch a flight back this weekend to visit her."

Daisy did not respond at first and then said, "You won't catch me flying. I don't fly. Not because of what happened on 9/11... I just don't fly."

Gladwin grinned and said, "Some people just don't fly, I understand. I flew helicopters during the Vietnam War."

Daisy let out an uncomfortable laugh at Gladwin's bravado and said, "That's even worse; you'll never catch me in a helicopter either."

She gently handed him the gift wrapped unicorn.

"I appreciate your time Ms. Acres, and it was nice to meet you."

Gladwin was about to exit when Daisy reminded him, "Ah, Detective, I don't want to have to call the police on you for shoplifting." She laughed and politely explained that the unicorn was actually $75 and that she would need $15 more.

Gladwin was embarrassed and instantly pulled out another $20. He then took back the cash and decided to spring his American Express. He signed, grabbed the receipt and said goodbye.

On his way out, Daisy asked him which hospital his sister was at in Detroit. He paused a moment and then answered "Saint John."

Gladwin walked back to the crowded lot behind the flower shop and got into his tan Sedan. He placed the box on the passenger side and pulled out the logbook from underneath his suit jacket. He rifled through it, scrutinizing the entries.

There was no documentation of the sunflower orders to Westwood Memorial or Hollywood Forever.

He placed a call to Agent Kim.

"Where are you?" Gladwin said.

"The OC, setting up for the Death Expo, remember?" Agent Kim said.

"What did you find out about Mike Maple?" Gladwin said.

"He's dead."

"Dead?"

"99 & 44/100% dead."

"How?"

"Heart attack two years ago."

"What? He was just in my office two days ago."

Gladwin's mind flashed to Maple sitting in front of him with the cheap gold urn in the Payless shoe box.

"That's because that wasn't Mike Maple," Agent Kim said. "That was Stan Glen."

This took a minute to penetrate Gladwin's mind. He hung up without saying goodbye and pulled out of the lot.

The sound of screeching tires woke him up from his daze as a gigantic Hummer nearly sent Gladwin to his pine box.

Gladwin hit the brakes.

The driver of the Humvee kept staring at Gladwin as he drove around him and floored it through a red light.

Chapter 21

THE 75th ANNUAL DEATH CARE EXPO
was being held at the Anaheim Convention Center in Orange County. The logic was that morticians could bring
along their families to sunny California, the sunlit mortuary, and enjoy a little business and pleasure— maybe even
shoot some golf and hit Disneyland. This year was a special occasion since the NMA had secured keynote speakers
and New York Times' best selling authors to discuss financial planning for death. There were also digital technology
and environmental conferences; one called: *"Going Green:
Promoting Sustainability After Death."*

Agent Kim walked away from the registration area
of the Anaheim Convention Center, examining the foldout map of the exhibitor locations. He placed his lanyard
around his neck and entered the convention center hall.

The vendors were already busy setting up and loading in
for the Death Expo Trade Show; morticians and entrepre-
neurs assembled their booths and hung banners as hi-lo
drivers buzzed back and forth with FedEx boxes and

equipment. Agent Kim's directive was simple: his unit would be posing as exhibitors and attendees for "Operation Coffin Nail" and their front company was *Slumber World Inc.,* specializing in the finest silk pillows and casket linings.

Agent Kim located their booth, #465, from the foldout map issued by the exhibitor services company: GDS. They strategically positioned their booth across from where Gilded Hearse, the pre-need company Dean had designated, was to set up at booth #466.

Agent Kim took a look at their two skirted tables and then looked around at the other enormous displays and booths. The noxious smell of glue and new carpet permeated the convention center. It was making Agent Kim nauseous. He needed a cigarette. He fantasized briefly about a John Woo slow motion style cinematic shootout with gangster morticians. He imagined himself like Yun-Fat Chow with dark shades and twin guns blazing.

Agent Kim loved the thrill of it.

He loved his job.

Back to reality.

He took a look at the FedEx boxes that were stacked by his table and decided to start setting up and playing the role of exhibitor. His department spent $12,000 on this facade just to exhibit at this show, and all they got was two crappy card tables with gaudy, bedraggled skirts and several VIP passes that included the esteemed keynotes. It was a waste of the department's money, no doubt.

He sliced open the first FedEx box and pulled out the assembly instructions for their pop-up stand. The task was overwhelming. It was the equivalent of assembling an Ikea living room. It was designed for any idiot, but you knew you were in for several hours of intense labor. And it sucked Swedish meatballs. He didn't have the patience. He wanted action. Where was the rest of his unit to help out? Why did Gladwin order such a complicated set up? He decided to go have a smoke. On the way out, he passed a vendor named: Mobile Mortuary. He stopped and talked to the president.

"What do you guys do?" Agent Kim said.

"We are a mobile phone company that allows photo filesharing for relatives that can't attend the funeral," the president of the company said. He also explained how it was "big" in China. He gave Agent Kim his business card and told him to come back and visit him tomorrow when the show starts. He walked away unsettled and looked up at the large hanging banners announcing the keynotes and book signings; hour long seminars and workshops with rags to riches authors pontificating about financial planning for death. It was depressing. It was now 4 pm. Set up time was to conclude at 7 pm. There was still no sign of the vendor Gilded Hearse. Booth #466 was vacant. Agent Kim went outside to check in with Gladwin. He lit up his cigarette, kicked his leg back up against the wall, pulled out his Blackberry and called him.

"G-man, the rest of my unit hasn't arrived... what's going on?"

Gladwin was stressed out and stuck in solid gridlock when he picked up.

"They know to be there Kim, hang tight," Gladwin

said, "I'm shadowing Dean. I was tipped off by our informant where he is headed."

"And where is that?"

"Egyptian Theatre in Hollywood. I've got things covered up here. The instructions are simple: when the cast of *Harold & Maude* show up tomorrow at the Anaheim Convention Center: Bust 'em."

"What's the code," Agent Kim said.

"Wild World," Gladwin said.

Gladwin also warned Agent Kim not to harm any civilians in the convention center and that this was not a John Woo film. This is the real deal... don't blow it.

Chapter 22

DEAN SAT IN THE BALCONY OF THE EGYPTIAN
Theatre during a rare screening of the 1951 version of *The Enforcer*, starring Humphrey Bogart. The restorated, black & white classic played to a half-full theater. Afterwards, the Egyptian was having a Q & A with some ancient cast member they dug up from the original film, but Dean was there to make the exchange. He watched two gangsters being interrogated on the big screen:

Bogart: "Who's the man you deliver the bodies to?"
Gangster: "The undertaker."
Dean laughed at the dialogue as he listened to the classic actors voices echo in the Egyptian.
Detective: "What undertaker?"
Gangster: "Our undertaker... he worked for us exclusive."
Detective: "What's his name?"
Gangster: "I dunno, we call 'em sad eyes."

Quincy sidled toward Dean and took a seat. He let out a big sigh as he plopped down. He was a big guy, looked like Bob Barker with shock white hair. Immaculately dressed— although the black trench coat was a bit much, Dean thought.

Quincy could hardly contain himself. He said, "Do you have the book?"

Dean didn't take his eyes off the screen and suggested Quincy do the same as he passed him the Memorial Guest Registry book.

"Is it all there?" Quincy said. "The money and the jewels?"

"Does the Queen Mary have ghosts?"

Quincy didn't get Dean's ribald sense of humor. Dean affirmed the registry book was everything.

"The procession is set up at Ascension in Orange County," Dean said. "They'll be on a wild goose chase, but it's a dead end to nowhere."

Quincy glanced up at Bogart on the screen and said, "They've been watching us the whole time."

Dean just nodded, matter of fact.

"Nice touch James," he said. "You're a clever guy." He did a mafia style gangster impersonation: "You fadder would be proud... He was one helluva guy. I still miss him to this day." He slapped Dean on the knee, clutching the book in his other hand. He placed the registry book in his black trench coat and sidled back out and left the theater.

On the way out Quincy stopped in front of the 'Coming Attractions' posters in the entrance of the Egyptian. He took a double take. The poster was of the real, legendary James Dean in *Giant*. Dean sprawled out with his legs crossed in the back of that car, just as cool as can be.

James Dean was the King of Cool.

After Quincy left the Egyptian, he turned left and headed west on the star-studded Hollywood Boulevard, walking toward the parking garage. He passed the Scientology building, avoiding eye contact with the clipboard toting screeners in front.

He made a left down the side street, looked over his shoulder once to assure he wasn't being followed, and then ducked into the staircase that connected to the parking garage. As he walked up the dimly lit, fluorescent staircase to the fourth floor where he had parked, he could hear the echo of car doors slamming and drunken kids laughing, beginning their evening of debauchery.

He reached the fourth floor and was about to turn the handle of the steel door, when he heard a deep voice that appeared to come out of nowhere, asking him to hand over the Memorial Guest Registry book. It was Detective Gladwin.

He froze.

He explained that it was in his trench coat and that he would gladly comply.

Gladwin asked him to remove his coat and slowly hand it over to him.

Quincy did exactly as he asked, a little too slow for Gladwin.

He felt the gun at his back and slowly unbuttoned the trench coat. Gladwin ripped it away from him and made sure the book was in the pocket by patting the jacket with his free hand.

Quincy could still hear the echo of people's voices and screeching rubber of tires against asphalt, as cars drove in and out.

He stood looking down, for what seemed to be forever, at the shit in the corner of the stairwell: the food wrappers, empty Red Bull canisters, piss and cigarette butts.

He glanced up at the blue graffiti on the door. The gang scrawling was greek to him, and all he could feel was an acute tinge of senselessness. A deadend rebellion.

That was the last thing he saw before three bullets hit him in the back.

Chapter **23**

BISHOP LOCATED A RENTAL HEARSE
online on Craigslist from some dude in Hawthorne. It was
going to cost him an extra $700 plus delivery charges to
their Mortuary, but he figured *Harold & Maude* was going to solve all of their financial woos, so he didn't mind
doling out the extra cash. Even if they trashed the hearse,
he figured they would have enough money to buy a whole
fleet of hearses when this caper was over.

Before he logged off the laptop, he opened up his Yahoo!
Messenger on his desktop. Bishop had instructed Stan
Glen to use OTR (Off The Record) plug-in that encrypts
IM messages. He said he would send him a fingerprint (a
string of numbers and letters that uniquely identify a key)
at approximately 7:30 p.m. They also agreed to speak in
code. Wes Bishop used "Mr. Bojangles" and Stan Glen
used "Lew Archer." This is what they IM'd:

   Mr. Bojangles: You there?
   Lew Archer: Yes ;)

Mr. Bojangles: Don't wink at me... it's gay.
Lew Archer: :(
Mr. Bojangles: You picked up the papers?
Lew Archer: Confirmed. I picked 'em up.
Mr. Bojangles: Then I'm ready to dance for you in worn out shoes.
Lew Archer: *Mr. Bojangles, Mr. Bojangles, Mr Bojangles, dance. Ha Ha.*
Mr. Bojangles: ThunderRoad tomorrow, that's where we switch.
Lew Archer: We'll meet at Heartattack and Vine when the show is over?
Mr. Bojangles: Screamin' Jay says everything is A-O-K on this end.
Lew Archer: What about Notorious R.I.P?
Mr. Bojangles: I Put a Spell On Him ;)
Lew Archer: (pause) Don't wink at me... it's gay.
Mr. Bojangles: Don't forget to bring an undertaker's friend.
Lew Archer: Sure, you bring the wooden kimonos.
Mr. Bojangles: Sayonara, baby.

Bishop signed off and shut down his laptop. He waltzed into the chapel and watched Don King putting the finishing touches on Ms. Clarke. He was finally convinced that maybe King had a point. It would look like business as usual if the detectives started snooping around.

Bishop said, "Okay, all of our problems are solved. I managed to find us a black hearse for tomorrow's heist... you believe I found it on Craigslist?"

King did not answer.

Bishop laughed and said, "Fuck those dumbass gangsters."

A loud crash startled them. It came from the other side of the chapel. It sounded like shattering glass. Rudolph went tearing off, snorting and growling in the direction of the crash.

Bishop looked at King and motioned him to keep quiet. He pulled out a .38 from his vest. He held the revolver like a pro, raised up to his head, and rounded the corner circumspect like Sammy Davis Jr., if he were a cop.

Rudolph was barking like crazy until one single gunshot silenced him.

Bishop looked back at King, fighting back tears, but appeared intrepid as he disappeared down the hallway.

This was not the first time Bishop and King's mortuary had been broken into, King thought— so don't panic. They lived in "the hood" and were frequently vandalized. They always had to scrub off or paint over the gang graffiti by taggers; cost them a small fortune over time. Then there were the homeless people that regularly sacked out on their property. One time the police came knocking on their door because they thought their mortuary was leaving dead bodies on the front lawn. As it turned out, it was just homeless people. The police said it looked like a scene from *Night of The Living Dead*.

King was startled by a door slamming and then four subsequent gunshots. They were rapid in sequence, like a machine gun. Then raucous laughter. He saw a flash of light from the hallway.

There was no movement for a few minutes. King waited for Bishop to emerge from the hallway.

"*Rat-a-tat-tat, tat-tat-tat like that...*" Cash sang as he entered the room.

"*...never hesitate to put a nigga on his back,*" Zip finished the rap lyric from Dr. Dre's *The Chronic* for him. They were high as hell on the chronic too. King's mind flashed to Bishop in a pool of blood. He stood with his arms reaching for the sky, a spatula in his right hand.

"Please," King said, "don't kill me."

Zip walked over to the George Foreman Grill, grabbed a nearby fork and started digging in. Wendall and Cash started looking around at Ms. Clark's set up. Cash flashed King a grimacing look.

"What the hellz goin' on in here?" Cash said. "Why chu havin' a bbq with a corpse?"

King started stammering.

"It's not a barbeque... it's ah, a theme... her family requested..."

Cash cut him off by shoving his Uzi up King's nostril.

"We expired yo' partner," he said, "cause he gave us an expired card."

"What?"

"The ATM card Smokey gave us."

Cash pistol-whipped King. King dropped to his knees sobbing, blood trickling down his forehead.

"Please... we have a heist going down tomorrow. Millions of dollars."

Cash thought about what Belle Isle told him at the Commerce Casino. He looked at Zip and Wendell. They nodded. Cash said, "Where's the sheeit goin' down?"

"Orange County," King stammered again, "Ascension Cemetery. The guys we deal with are expecting us tomorrow morning to pick up the money... You kill me and we all lose out."

"Get a good, long look at this," Cash said as he passed King the Poloroid he just snapped of Bishop. King glanced at the photo and grimaced. There was Bishop, worse than he imagined, lying flat on his back in a pool of blood with several black holes in his suit. He had a contorted expression on his face. King closed his eyes momentarily and silently said to himself, "God help me."

"If yo' lyin' to me," Cash said, "then you end up like him."

He got right in King's face, grabbed him by the back of his collar and dug the Uzi into his cheek.

King shook his head no. The sweat poured down his cheeks. He said, "I swear to God, I would not be lying to you about this."

Cash released his grip. He took an apple from the picnic basket and chomped down, grinning with his big gold tooth gleaming and said to his posse, "It looks like we got ourselves a driver."

Those words were more terrifying than the Polaroid of Bishop. King's mind flashed to the long, horrific trek on the 405 Freeway which he never drove and avoided his whole life in California. He couldn't tell these street thugs he suffered from highway anxiety; they would laugh their gangster asses off. He weighed each of his excuses:

Excuse #1: He didn't have a driver's license. No. He

gave it to them when they jacked the hearse. Excuse #2: He had some medical condition. No. They wouldn't give a shit and weren't going to buy into that. Excuse #3: He was horrible with directions and Wes Bishop was supposed to be the driver. No way in hell. They would just tell him where to go.

Conclusion: He was fucked.

He had to face the fear and stay in the far right lane. He could get shitfaced, but then the paranoia crept in. If he was drunk or drove too slow, that would draw the attention of the Highway Patrol and fuck everything up with the heist. It was lose/lose. If he got pulled over with a hearse-load of Crenshaw gangsters, how in the hell was he going to talk his way out of that. Oddly enough, he wished they' would've shot him instead of Bishop.

He was already feeling dizzy just thinking about it.

Chapter 24

GLADWIN DROVE THROUGH THE GATES
of Hollywood Forever ostensibly to investigate and corroborate Daisy Acres' story. He noticed a large group of people carrying folding chairs and picnic baskets. He drove up and asked the guard on duty what was going on. Fireworks? The guard explained to Gladwin that it was "movie night" and asked Gladwin if he would like to buy a ticket. Gladwin said "sure" and made some idle conversation. He interviewed the guard about his recent memory of events and asked him if he recalled any deliveries from Daisy Acres Floral Shop. The guard told him he sees a lot of traffic these days since they put the 'Hollywood' back into 'Forever.' Gladwin concluded his interview and parked behind a purple hearse near the circular driveway.

He tucked the Memorial Guest Registry book under the front seat for safekeeping and threw Quincy's black trench coat over his arm like a waiter. He followed the direction of the crowd to the side of the building where the screening was taking place. He ditched the black trench coat over by Bugsy Siegel's grave. He figured he could pin Quincy's murder on the Smothers Brothers. When he got back into his car, he pulled out the registry book and examined the entries. He scanned three pages until he fixed on one egregious entry:

Peg Entwistle   *Holl**Y**woodland*   *9/29/1975*

Gladwin placed a call back to his office and asked them to run a search on the name: Peg Entwistle. Time was running out. He had Agent Kim covering *Harold & Maude* down in Orange County, but the real *Harold & Maude's* whereabouts remained obscured. He circled back around the cemetery and slowly passed by the graveside audience intently watching the screening of Billy Wilder's *Some Like it Hot* on the side of a mausoleum. He laughed to himself: "movie night." He took note of the Goths on the way out. He thought that one girl bared a strong resemblance to Maila Nurmi from Ed Wood's *Plan 9 From Outer Space*. He remembered what a shitty film *Plan 9* was and kept laughing at "movie night" in a graveyard. Great place for a date. As he drove back out through the gates, he was laughing so hard his eyes were tearing.

Manfred O and Gilda Hearse would've camped out at Hollywood Forever if the park's security didn't come around with their flashlights and patrol car, rousting everybody out. Manfred personally had all the time in the world since he was out of a job when Tower Records on Sunset permanently closed its doors. On their exit out, Gilda noticed the abandoned, cool black trench coat lying by Bugsy Siegel's grave. She tried it on and modeled it for Manfred, spinning around and batting her eyelashes. "You like?" She teased in a dark, commanding tone.

Manfred grinned, exposing his cosmetic vampire fangs. As they reached the purple hearse, she pulled out a folded piece of paper and a laminated badge from the inside of the trench coat. The expo badge read:

Ray Driscol
Wayne County Coroner
Attendee
The 75th Annual Death Care Expo

She then pulled out a Yahoo map of Ascension Cemetery in Orange County and a scrawled note.

It read: *Harold & Maude opens this Friday.*

What serendipity. How fucking cool is that?

She explained to Manfred what it meant: They could attend the Death Expo at the Anaheim Convention Center and afterwards catch a screening of *Harold and Maude* at Ascension Cemetery. They both loved *Harold and Maude* and had seen it at least 50 times, but never saw it screened in a cemetery. They figured it would be crowded, so they decided to head down to OC to check it out and spend the night— Sometimes they would sleep in the back of the hearse. It was cheaper than a motel and more romantic.

Before they hit the 405 Freeway to Orange County, they stopped at Helter Skelter, an alternative Goth club located in Hollywood. They decided to have several drinks and trance dance to the electronic sounds of the *Sisters of*

Mercy, Type O Negative and Marilyn Manson. They spread the word at Helter Skelter about the screening of *Harold and Maude* and explained that it was going to be a sold out crowd at the cemetery.

Chapter **25**

DEAN SAT ALONE AT THE DAKOTA
restaurant located in the Hollywood Roosevelt. He put
aside the cryptogram puzzle he was working on from the
Penny Press magazine and ordered another glass of mer-
lot. He pulled out a file from his nearby briefcase, another
aged photo of his father's charred hearse and Stan Glen's
report from *Operation Grim Reaper.* It read:

OGR-29SEPT75:

   *"We observed Frank DeRossa, aka "Big Frank," walking
to the black hearse with his son, James DeRossa, shortly after
the Illych family Russian wake. This was at approximately
19:01 hours. Our informant, Ray Driscol, a Wayne County
Coroner, had been on the inside for no more than 20 minutes and observed the alleged decedent, Ivan Illych (casket was
closed). He had also noted that Big Frank had passed his son,
James, the Memorial Guest Registry book and replaced it with
an identical book. Ray Driscol signed the book under the*

alias, Nicolas Ray, and stated to my partner, Mike Maple, and I that the book's entries were not full and there was no reason to replace the book. Furthermore, Driscol had identified several known crime family members and did not see their names reflected in the registry. It was at that moment that Ray Driscol was asked to leave and was escorted out of the wake. The pallbearers brought out the casket at approximately: 19:21 hours and rear loaded it into Big Frank's black hearse. His son, James, was about to get into the hearse when he ran back into DeRossa & Son's Mortuary. Big Frank got in the driver's side of the hearse and there was a huge explosion. It was obviously rigged. James emerged moments later from the funeral home holding a magazine. I immediately called the Detroit Fire Department. The blast had ripped apart the hearse, injuring and killing several nearby attendees who were later rushed to St. John's Hospital. It was later discovered that the C-4 explosive device was embedded in the casket of the decedent and detonated by a nearby car (that device or suspect was never located). "Operation Grim Reaper" also revealed that the decedent was a John Doe and no solid leads have been provided as to his identity.

Conclusion: The Russian Maffiya had planted the explosive device and had orchestrated the hit on Big Frank on the evening of September 29th, 1975. Big Frank had been accused of stealing from the Russians during the Windsor Raceway heist."

Signed: Detective Stan Glen

Dean put the report and photo back into the file and placed it back in his briefcase. He paused and then pulled out his Blackberry and placed a call. A woman's voice answered.

"It's time to roll *Harold & Maude*," Dean said.

The voice on the other end laughed.

He grinned and continued with the instructions. "The procession has been set up and it's payback time. We'll meet at the Y tomorrow."

"*It's a Mad, Mad, Mad, Mad World,*" the voice on the other end said.

Dean joked, "*Baby, Baby, It's a Wild World,* quoting Cat Stevens.

"At least with *Harold & Maude* in it," she said.

"See you tomorrow," Dean said.

Dean hung up and returned to his cryptogram puzzle. He had ample time for games. Truth of the matter was, he was financially set the minute he left Jackson County. Big Frank had left him his entire estate in a trust and his attorney had held all of the assets in a bank account for James while he was in prison. He only cared about one thing when he got out: getting even with the people responsible for his father's death.

Chapter **26**

"IT'S LIKE EL MARIACHI IN A CASKET, HUH,"
Joe Smothers joked with the man only known as 'Juan.' Joe
inspected the contents of the gaudy, chartreuse casket. It
was an arsenal of AK-47s, shotguns, .38s, .357 Magnums
and a half-dozen grenades thrown in as a bonus. Juan explained to him, in broken English, that there was no way to
trace the weapons and that the guns were smuggled in by a
reputable landscaping company. It cost Joe two expensive
Batesvilles, $4K in cash, and a future promise to smuggle
in some illegals from Honduras. Joe paid Juan lip service
on the last promise. He rushed Juan along, knowing Vic
would pull up any minute. They shook hands and Juan
climbed back into his Ryder truck, never to be seen again.

Joe was the agenté funeraio in this crazy procesíon and
knew he had made a deal with diablo: Gladwin, that is.
"Jesus," he mumbled to himself. "This is as insane as those
North Hollywood bank robber nuts back in '94." He knew
that bringing this kind of heavy artillery to the party was a

recipe for disaster and that he was even putting Vic at risk, but what other choice did he have.

Vic pulled up in the white hearse moments later to find Joe sealing the chartreuse casket. Joe instructed him to rear it in so that they could load in the dummy caskets. Vic got out and started in on the comments and questions.

"That is one ugly casket."

"It's the cheapest one. What do you expect," Joe said.

"We'll probably get pulled over and issued a ticket for this eyesore," Vic said. He opened the back of the white hearse.

"What do you want to do," Joe said, "use the most expensive box for the job?"

Vic and Joe grabbed the casket by the handles and lifted it off the two wooden saw horses. Vic nearly broke his back. He dropped his side back down.

"Jesus," he said, "it's fucking heavy. Did the manufacturer deliver it with a body?" Vic rested against the casket and exhaled. He was ready to open it when Joe brushed away his hands.

"It's protection. Forget about what's inside."

"What's inside?"

"It doesn't matter what's inside, let's load it in and call it a night. We've got an early morning tomorrow."

Joe did not have the patience for Vic's questions and did not want him nosing around in his coffin war chest. He also did not have the heart to tell him that the contents of the casket might keep him out of jail and that he was doing this for his little brother. He was going out blazing. Joe laid on the charm and put his arm around Vic's shoulder, turning him away from the casket.

"Vic," he said, "you remember the first time we were mystery shopped?"

Vic laughed and said, "How could I forget. It was a casket like this that cost us the fine." He jerked his thumb back at the chartreuse casket.

"Precisely," Joe said.

"I shoulda known when that old bag kept asking about the teal casket in the back of our parlor and why it wasn't displayed in front with the others."

"And you challenged her," Joe said, "about the book-stores and grocery stores. It was comical."

Vic thought about it and started laughing.

"Yeah, yeah I still think it's bullshit that that became part of the FTC's Funeral Rule," Vic said, "that the cheapest casket has to be grouped in with the expensive caskets, and that our industry would get fined for not complying. I mean, how is it any different than when grocery stores place all the high-priced items at eye-level and the best deals on the top and bottom shelves where customers are less likely to look?"

"It's called product placement," Joe said.

Joe looked around the U-Store-It industrial facility and turned to Vic and said, "What the hell's the matter with us, Vic? Being reduced to a shed in a storage facility... we deserve better than this. When we started this thing I thought we were going to be the Costco of casket shop-ping and eventually grow into the WalMart of the funeral industry, but we aren't making it. I'm ready to close the shed door for good on Coffin Depot."

"We do need to build our business back up," Vic said, "It takes a while."

"Three years?" Joe said in a sobering tone. "I think that's long enough. I'm finished after tomorrow when we hit pay dirt."

After a few minutes of silence, Vic said, "Do you really think we can trust this Dean guy?"

"No, but I'm willing to take the drive and one day out of my mundane life to find out."

"What if we're being set up?"

"It's a little too late to be asking that question, isn't it? Besides, look at it this way. We're used to set ups with mystery shoppers. We're just dropping some caskets off like we're asked to and headin' down to the Death Expo. I'm just arming myself with the every man for himself attitude." A little Freudian slip from Joe Smothers' mouth. He couldn't look Vic in the eyes.

Vic said, "Well you know what they say: 'Don't do the crime, if you can't pay the time.'"

"Yeah right, save that horseshit for Hollywood. You want to hire a hitman these days, hire a celebrity to do the job. They get away with murder."

They both laughed and returned to loading the casket.

Vic nearly broke his balls after they slid it in and asked again, "So what's in the casket?"

Joe rotated his neck from side-to-side to relieve the tension and said, "Sand bags, brother... I'm expecting a big storm tomorrow."

Vic still didn't believe his brother, but he kept the lid closed to save face.

Chapter 27

THE EL TORO "Y" IS ONE THE BUSIEST
interchanges in the world. It's where the Santa Ana Freeway, Interstate 5, and the San Diego Freeway, Interstate
405, merge. This morning it would be on every news channel in Southern California and establish an all time record
for congestion. Skycam 9 loaded up their gear and set out
for the morning's SigAlerts.

A pimped-out black hearse could be seen driving at
a snails pace, hugging the right hand lane, at the break
of dawn. Cash and his g-sters had pimped out the hearse
MTV style. They transformed the coach at a local chop-
shop, slapped on some gold rims, added tinted windows
and changed the license plate on the rear. It now read:
Deathrow. There was also spray painted gang graffiti on
the side of the hearse. Cash would deal with those 'mutha-
fuckas' responsible for tagging it after the heist.

Don King had driven over 70 anxiety-ridden miles and

was now drenched in sweat from head to toe. The freeway was like a roller coaster to him, but worse with a gun at the back of his neck. He was a basket case the whole trip. Cash kept prodding him, "C'mon... step on it, man." He would dig the glock deeper into King's neck and ask, "What's wrong wit 'chu anyway? Man, you drive like my grandma." King never went over 45 m.p.h. "It's a funeral," King said. "We're supposed to drive slow."

Cash warned King that it was his funeral if he didn't step on it. He continued to joke around with his posse and lit up another joint. King was getting stoned just breathing the air.

The black hearse slowed down to about a 15 m.p.h. crawl when King noticed the line of hearses forming outside the gates of Acsension.

The g-sters looked at him for an explanation.

Meanwhile, Agent Kim was about to check out of the Double Tree Hotel and head over to the Death Expo when he got a frantic call from his surveillance unit that was staked out at Ascension. Their recorded cell phone conversation went as follows:

Agent Sweetzer: "Agent Kim, how many hearses are there supposed to be?"

Agent Kim: (long pause) "Three. One black. One White. One Silver. Why?"

Agent Sweetzer: "Ah, we got sort of a problem then..."

Agent Kim: "What sort of a problem?"

Agent Sweetzer: "We're here and there are about 20 hearses of various colors in line at the gates of Ascension.

Please advise."

Agent Kim: "Stay put 'til I make a call."

Kim hung up, confused. He placed a call to Gladwin, but G-Man was incommunicado. He left a message explaining the new twist and asked G-Man to advise him of his next move. He got a call back, but it was Agent Sweetzer calling again.

Agent Sweetzer: "Agent Kim, it looks like the superintedent or gatekeeper is turning the hearses away from the gates. They appear to be arguing."

Agent Kim: "Can you get a look at the driver or other drivers?"

Agent Sweetzer: "It's a woman... she looks like Elvira."

Agent Sweetzer zoomed in with his binoculars on the other hearse drivers right to left, then left to right.

Agent Kim: "Well?"

Agent Sweetzer: "Dunno, it looks like a Halloween party."

Agent Kim: "Never mind that, don't lose sight of *Harold & Maude* when they dig 'em up. Be ready to roll."

Agent Kim hung up and headed over to the Anaheim Convention Center.

King and the g-sters watched the throng of goth hearses slowly pull out from the gates. As soon as it was clear, Cash dug the glock into King's neck and barked at him to move up to the gates.

The black hearse was greeted by the superintendent on duty. He referenced some notes and a photo of Bishop & King that was given to him by Dean. King checked out, but

130

he thought the g-sters were questionable. He looked at the *Deathrow* license plate and gave King a reproving look. King assured him they were there to see the real *Harold & Maude,* and he was handed a beautiful bouquet of sunflowers through the window. The superintendent pointed to the throng of goth hearses, now parked along the side of the cemetery gates; the goths were outside the hearses congregating, scheming. He laughed at them, shrugging his shoulders, and explained they thought *Harold and Maude* was being screened there tonight and came to buy tickets this morning. "Imagine that." He nervously unlocked the gate and waved the black hearse through.

That's when Cash fired three shots into him as they pulled through the gates. He said, "We are the only ones here to see *Harold & Maude,* you stupid muthafucka."

King hit the brakes.

He sat motionless as he watched the life bleed out of the superintendent through the rearview mirror.

Before he could say, "FUCK," a white hearse rear ended the black hearse and thrust everyone forward.

Cash's glock flew out of his hands and hit the front windshield. This was followed by a thunderous crack and the back and side windows of the black hearse being blown out from a shotgun. It splattered Wendall's head like a tomato and covered the interior with shards of glass, blood and skull fragments. Sunflower petals were floating everywhere like feathers from a pillow. King's only reaction was to put the pedal to the floor.

"Move it, man. Move it." Cash said.

The black hearse burned rubber and peeled out.

Agent Sweetzer gave the signal from inside his surveillance SUV and shouted, *"It's a wild world."*

He shouted again, *"I REPEAT, IT'S-A-WILD-WORLD... Harold & Maude* is in progress. Shots fired."

Two black SUVs were now headed straight on towards the black and white hearses; these were the FBI undercover calvary.

Zip braced himself and leaned out the left side of the blown out hearse window. He unloaded several rounds into the oncoming SUVs from his Uzi.

Joe Smothers kept firing at the back of the black hearse while Vic had a death grip on the wheel of the white hearse. He watched Joe reach into the casket and pull out an AK-47.

"What the fuck is going on?" Vic said.

"It's us or them, little brother." Joe said, "And I know for goddamn sure it ain't us. I'd rather be in that box back there than to serve one day in prison."

Vic glanced at Joe holding the AK-47 out the window.

King was freaking out and swerving all over the inside road of Ascension Cemetery. The white hearse kept firing and missing the unsteady target. King glanced down at the glock resting on the passenger side floorboard. Cash had now crawled through to the back of the hearse and was firing on the Smothers Brothers with the .44 Magnum that he had pried out of Wendall's dead hand. Both hearses were pushing 80 m.p.h and were headed straight for the back gates of Ascension. The two SUVs that Zip had fired on sped off in opposite directions out of the line of fire.

King could see the back gates closed up ahead and was running out of road. For no logical reason at all, he swerved left and jumped the curb, clipping the side of an elaborate mausoleum which catapulted Zip out of the window and onto the lawn. Cash's body slammed back and forth against the inside of the hearse.

King hit the brakes, leaving tire tracks in the grass for at least 50 feet. Cash was floating and slamming around the back, obeying and disobeying the laws of gravity. The black hearse spun sideways. King grabbed the glock from the floorboard and spun around in his seat, screaming like a wild Indian until he unloaded every last bullet into Cash's gansta body.

The white hearse was charging like a bull and was about to broadside King until King snapped out of killer mode and into Mario Andretti mode. He revved the engine, turned the hearse around and then plowed straight through the back fencing of the cemetery, the white hearse missing him by inches and fishtailing behind him.

The FBI SUVs followed in hot pursuit, spitting grass behind them.

The silver Big Sleep hearse drove slowly through the gates. It stopped momentarily to view the dead superintendent and then accelerated in the direction of the skid marks and bullet riddled headstones.

Sirens could be heard in the distance.

The silver hearse idled for a moment by the mausoleum that King had just taken a chunk out of.

Zip sprung up on the driver's side of the silver hearse and stuck his Uzi in the face of the Big Sleep driver, who was not Coffin Joe.

"Get the fuck ott' the hearse," Zip said.

"It's yours, take it man." The Big Sleep driver was early 50's, overweight and donning a salt & pepper rug that he must have found at a discount wig shop on Hollywood Boulevard. He raised his chubby fingers in the air, being careful not to make eye contact with Zip.

Zip shouted, "Are you a cop?"

The Big Sleep driver pleaded, "No. I'm covering shifts for a guy named Coffin Joe from our company... He gave me an extra $500... Please, I don't know what the hell is going on here. I was told to pick up a tourist this morning that would be waiting at the Nicole Simpson grave and that we would head back to Westwood Memorial. I thought it might be you.

The blood was stinging Zip's eyes and all he could hear were more gunshots, squealing tires and sirens looming closer. He said, "Why the fuck would that be me, fat man?"

Zip grabbed the Big Sleep driver by his wig. It came off in his hands. He looked at it for a moment, then back at the driver's bald head. He threw the wig on the mausoleum, cracked the driver in the head, and then forced his way in the silver hearse. He twisted the keys in the ignition and took off like a bat out of hell after the other hearses. The Big Sleep driver sat disoriented on the curb, not understanding what the hell just happened, when a purple hearse sped up in front of the mausoleum. It was followed by a procession of other gothic hearses.

Gilda stuck her head out. She was visibly upset. "Hey, do you know what happened back there? She said. "We came to get tickets for a screening of *Harold and Maude* and now the dude at the gate is dead. Do you know if they will have a screening later?"

The Big Sleep driver did not comprehend her question, not because of the crack on the head and possible concussion, but because it just wasn't making any fucking sense. Was she joking?

"You mean the movie, *Harold and Maude?*"

"What else would I be referring to?" She noticed the blood trickling down his forehead. He seemed disoriented. "Are you okay?" "Do you need an ambulance or something?"

"My hearse was just jacked..." he said, "stolen... my boss is going to kill me."

News choppers were flying overhead and now descending closer. The Big Sleep driver rose to his feet, unsteady, and walked towards the purple hearse. He looked back at the line of hearses and their freakish occupants. He shielded his eyes, looking up at the news choppers. He said, "Can you give me a ride back to LA?"

Gilda looked back at Manfred who flashed his cosmetic fangs. He nodded yes. The Big Sleep driver thanked them and crawled in the rear of the hearse. Manfred asked him if they had any job openings for drivers at The Big Sleep. The purple hearse followed the skid marks out the back of Ascension Cemetery and onto the 405 Freeway.

Skycam 9 was just about to go over the morning

SigAlerts when it spotted the high speed procession. From their perspective they could see the black, white and silver color vehicles moving at high speeds. This was good. They knew that ever since the Juice was loose in '94 they still got good ratings when it came to high speed chases and the LA Mayor knew it too. One car was newsworthy, but three? They cut to broadcast right away.

"Folks, this is Skycam 9," the pilot said. "Looks like we have another high-speed chase on the 405 headed Northbound to the El Toro Y."

They dropped down lower...

"...Looks to be three SUVs, maybe larger... Yukon XL's..."

They dropped lower...

"There's three of them... Cadillac Escalandes... CHP is on the scene flanking them."

The news chopper dropped even lower, zooming in even closer with their cameras.

"No, looks like they could be Hummers... a white one... followed by a silver one... WHOA. The silver one just rammed the black one. Holy (bleep)." THERE ARE THREE HEARSES. Not sure if this is in fact a funeral procession, but we are seeing the CHP in hot pursuit."

The cameraman in Skycam 9 tapped the pilot and pointed downward in a forceful manner. He pointed his camera in a backwards direction. There was another high-speed procession gaining on the other three hearses and CHP. The purple hearse was in the lead followed by even more hearses of various colors, and they were gaining on the procession. The Skycam pilot said, "I can tell you at this point, this is no funeral... not at these speeds. We will keep you posted on this exciting story breaking out of Orange County on the 405 Freeway."

Chapter **28**

THE FAMOUS HOLLYWOOD SIGN on Mount Lee loomed high above the serene, circular foothills of Beachwood Canyon Drive. Another silver Big Sleep hearse could be seen winding up the road. It parked roughly 100 yards from the sign. A tourist got out to snap photos.

The driver noticed the silver landau bar was hanging by a screw. Kids were always stealing them.

A gust of wind made him grab his chauffeur's cap. The whir of an R-44 sightseeing helicopter cast a shadow as it swooped over the roof of the hearse. It was flying a little too low, in his opinion.

He watched it lift towards the Hollywood sign and circle around the back, hovering over the Y. Gladwin sat inside the helicopter opposite the pilot, pretending to be interested in the tourist map. He tossed the map on the floorboard of the luxury cabin and pulled his gun.

"Drop the bird behind the hearse."

The pilot's mind flashed to terrorism in a nanosecond, even though Gladwin didn't look Middle Eastern or fit the profile.

"What the hell is going on?" The pilot said. "If you think you're going to crash this chopper into that sign, you're crazy..." He clutched the throttle tighter.

"I'm getting dizzy." Gladwin lied. "Just drop this goddamn bird behind the silver hearse like I asked you."

He flashed the pilot his badge. The pilot was somewhat relieved and complied with Gladwin's order.

The helicopter touched down approximately 20 yards behind the hearse. The Big Sleep tourist clutched his Star Map as the blades of the chopper blew every scrap of debris and litter in all directions. The Big Sleep driver jumped back behind the wheel of the hearse. The helicopter cut it's engine.

Gladwin said to the pilot, "It's a beautiful day, go take a hike."

The pilot hesitated for a moment, sensing something was not quite right. Gladwin watched the pilot's eyes and his hands closely. He could see him thinking about grabbing his gun.

"It's a sting operation, move it," he said. "Don't worry about your property, I'll have it safely returned to your company."

"It's my property and my company," the pilot said.

Gladwin wasn't impressed. He kept staring down the pilot to move along.

The pilot begrudgingly began his long walk downhill.

Gladwin waited until he completely vanished before he approached the silver hearse. He slowly crept up on the side and leveled his gun at the driver, who was thumbing through a book. He warned the tourist to freeze. The tourist screamed and dropped his Star Map; his back to Gladwin with his hands reaching for the sky.

Gladwin pulled out the black Memorial Guest Registry book and opened it up to a page with a yellow Post It.

"Clever, DeRossa," he said, "real clever." Gladwin moved closer to the driver's side of the silver hearse and said, "Peg Entwistle. The only guest that night that didn't check out in your little black book. I figured it out."

He placed his hand on the handle of the driver's side door.

"You almost got away with it," Gladwin said, "except Driscol—" he laughed under his breath, "Quincy gave me the book." So the money is right up there." He glanced up at the Y of the Hollywood sign.

"Peg Entwistle, the 1930's actress who jumped 50 feet to her death." He stared at the scrawled signature that indicated *Peg Entwistle from HollYwoodland*, as they used to call it prior to 1945.

The Y was underlined.

He clutched the Memorial Guest Registry book, moved toward the silver hearse and said, "I hope you brought some shovels with you because after I unearth the loot, I'm gonna bury you."

Gladwin narrowed his eyes at the driver, slack jawed. He asked him to get out of the car.

The driver got out slowly.

It was not James DeRossa, aka "James Dean..." it was a complete stranger. He stared at the driver completely addled and said, "Who the hell are you?"

"Tom Rose, sir." The driver said. "I'm an employee of Big Sleep Celebrity Death Tours and I don't know anything about any money."

He stood perplexed, fixated on the gun.

Gladwin looked at the tourist for an explanation.

"I'm Mike Martino from Michigan, sir." The tourist replied. "Just came here to see the—" Gladwin cut him off and thought to himself: if it's not the El Toro Y and it's not here underneath the Y of the Hollywood sign, then where the hell is the money?

His mind was racing; he had reached another deadend.

He told the Big Sleep driver and his tourist to beat it. Take a hike. Leave the keys in the hearse. The driver complied and said he didn't want any trouble. He and his tourist followed the vertiginous road downhill, no questions asked.

Gladwin was now sweating profusely. He stared at the abandoned helicopter and empty hearse. He began to feel those sharp, shooting chest pains again. Damned Amazon.com. Where was his fucking Philips Heartstart Home Automated External Defibrillator? He paid extra for 2nd Day Air.

If he was fabricating his vertigo in the helicopter, he was certainly feeling it now. He tossed the black Memorial Guest Registry book in the back of the hearse and got in the driver's side.

Useless. Another dead end.

Quincy came to mind. The poor bastard lost his life over a hoax. The police have probably found his corpse in that stinking stairwell by now. The James Dean connection resurfaced again. He wondered why DeRossa would come into town under that name? Go through all that trouble. The smokescreen just didn't make any sense. DeRossa's father left him the death care business, but DeRossa had rejected it. He claimed he didn't want any part of it. His father left him money in a trust. So James DeRossa blows into town as James Dean for a week, sets up a caper with these other merchants of death, but he is the rebel without a corpse. Gladwin laughed to himself. Rebel without a corpse.

He started feeling that squeezing, tight pain in his chest again. Why did he put off scheduling his 64-slice CT Scan?

His cell phone rang. It was Agent Kim, adrenaline pumping.

"G-man, are you near a TV?"

"Why would I be in front of a TV, Agent Kim?" Gladwin said.

"I'm watching it on my mobile phone as we speak, it's unreal."

"Watching what?" Gladwin could not stand how Agent Kim would always beat around the bush. He sat on the curb, dejected, rubbing his chest. "What's unreal?"

"The high-speed chase at the Y," Agent Kim said.

"Why aren't you at the Convention Center?" Gladwin said.

"I am at the convention center."

"Well, do you mind telling me what the hell is happening there?"

"Nothing. Not a damn thing."

"Nothing?"

"Gilded Hearse never showed up," Agent Kim said. "All the action is going down at the El Toro Y. I'm watching it on my mobile phone."

Gladwin was completely confused. He said, "The money is there after all?"

"Nah, nothing was disinterred. It was a blood bath before anyone could grab a shovel and dig in."

"Speak fucking English."

"They killed the superintendent—"

"Who's 'they?'"

"King shot 'em according to our agents."

"Where's Bishop?"

"We don't know yet, but he didn't make it to the heist. King brought some gangbangers with him instead. Maybe a double-cross. We don't know who they are, or why they are driving with him or what connection they might have with *Harold & Maude*, if any."

Gladwin paused a moment then said, "The Smothers Brothers?"

"They're pushing 90 on the 405 with King and the g-sters."

"Wait a minute," Gladwin said, "they're in the same hearse?"

"No, G-man. Different hearses, same high-speed chase. In fact there are now about 20 hearses in this chase."

"20 hearses?"

"Yeah, these other freaks showed up asking about *Harold & Maude* before the super went down. We don't know who they are or why they were dressed up for Halloween."

Gladwin's blood was boiling. He looked at the Big Sleep logo on the side of the silver hearse.

"Is Coffin Joe down there?

"Yes, a silver hearse has been identified in the pursuit."

"So no money and jewels has been recovered?"

"Like I said, G-man, there was a blood bath at the cemetery before anyone could break out their shovels."

"Dean?"

"No sign of 'em. Do you have mobile television?"

Gladwin thought about breaking out the booze at this point. "No Kim," he said, "I don't watch TV on my fucking phone... who has time for that shit? Listen, you stay put down there and make sure you nab Maple—"

"You mean, Stan Glen," Agent Kim said.

"Glen. Whatever... just fucking nab the whole lot of them and any other conspirators at the expo."

"Any luck on your end G-man?"

"I'm following up on some leads" Gladwin said.

He hung up on Agent Kim. He was on borrowed time. While the units were in place at the Anaheim Convention Center, he had to find Dean, kill him and recover the real *Harold & Maude*... if there was such a thing. Gladwin was beginning to wonder.

He placed a call to the Hollywood Roosevelt and was informed that Dean had checked out hours ago. He climbed into the silver hearse and revved it up. He looked over his shoulder a few times, spooked. He kept imagining a casket in the back with a decedent. His mind was playing tricks on him. He pictured himself inside that casket in the back of the hearse. Then about being hauled to his grave by a hearse. His last ride. The whole thing creeped him out. He was giving himself the willies. He put it in drive and headed back down the canyon to talk to the owner of *The Big Sleep Celebrity Death Tours*. He thought about the only positive thing a hearse had to offer was that you could blow red lights, but then again you had to be hauling a body. He didn't have one to haul. Yet.

He drove past the sightseeing pilot and the Big Sleep driver and his tourist. He heard a couple of "heys" and "stops," but ignored them and drove on.

Quincy's cell phone rang. Gladwin picked it up and just listened. The caller said "hello." That was his mistake.

Gladwin knew it was Stan Glen. He figured Glen must be meeting up with DeRossa.

He would kill them both.

On the drive back Gladwin thought about Spencer Tracy in *It's a Mad, Mad, Mad, Mad World,* and how all those crazy people were chasing the Smilers' money that was buried under the elusive "W" in Santa Rosita Park. Jimmy Durante's voice echoed in his mind saying it's under the big "Dubya."

The big Dubya...

Where the hell is it?

Gladwin began to wonder if the *Operation Grim Reaper* tapes were just a ruse. Maybe there was no "Y." He pulled into the *The Big Sleep Celebrity Death Tours* office lot. It was located on the corner of Franklin and Vine next to a tire shop. The owner came out yelling at Gladwin.

"Where the hell have you been?" He said. His next question was: "Who the hell are you?" Followed by: "Where is Tom Rose, the driver?"

Gladwin got out of the hearse and pulled out his badge. The Big Sleep owner stepped back, almost ready to dart.

"Hey look," the owner said, "I don't know what Mr. Rose did, or what he is involved in, but I run a clean business here..."

"This isn't about Tom Rose," Gladwin said. "Does this guy work for you?"

Gladwin produced a photo and showed it to the owner. It was of Coffin Joe at Westwood Memorial, letting his tourists out of the silver hearse.

The owner strained at the picture.

"I'm afraid I don't recognize him," he said.

Gladwin suggested he try harder.

"Look, I have four drivers," he said. "Three men. One woman. And none of them resemble that driver." He laughed.

Gladwin took down all of their names on his Steno pad: Tom Rose. Todd Singer. Marcus Helms. Jackie Antos. Gladwin looked up from the note pad and said, "Notice anything odd or unusual about these drivers over the past week, like changes in behavior, route or tardiness?"

"The drivers usually work out shift changes with each other," he said. "If one of them wants a day off, another driver will cover their shift."

"Where is Todd Singer?" Gladwin asked.

"He's right over there sleeping in the back of the hearse."

Gladwin glanced over at yet another silver hearse. He thought: that leaves Marcus and Jackie. He stared at the photo again. Was Coffin Joe down in OC? He stared at Coffin Joe's photo, the mop of hair and bushy stash. His suit was baggy. Who was he? She?

What was Dean's connection to him? Her?

He asked the owner if he would mind giving him a lift back to the FBI office in Westwood.

The owner said "sure" and even offered to throw in a complimentary tour on the drive there.

Chapter **29**

THE CHP FINALLY USED THE PIT MANEUVER on the silver hearse after the purple hearse moved out of their way and pulled off to the right shoulder of the 405 Freeway. The silver hearse spun around facing oncoming traffic. Cars were swerving and crashing everywhere. The repeated sounds of tires skidding and metal crunching could be heard for at least a mile.

"It was the most terrifying thing I had ever experienced in my entire life," one of the motorists would later say. "We see these chases everyday on the news, but when you're actually involved... and it's hearses... at those speeds... it's just an image you won't ever forget... it was horrific."

News coverage from Skycam 9 caught the white hearse hitting a spike strip and skidding to a stop. Joe Smothers eventually had a stand-off with officers. Skycam 9 cut to commercial due to the violent ending. Joe Smothers kept pulling out more weapons from his casket arsenal while Vic kept screaming he was innocent, until they finally shot the hell out of both of them... The Smothers Brothers were pronounced dead at the scene.

Don King finally came to a dead-end and solid stop after he took the service drive for several miles and led the CHP into a residential cul-de-sac in Irvine— another news channel covered this less interesting story. When the police apprehended King he was petrified, drenched in sweat, and his hands had to be pried off the steering wheel. Although he finally complied with the CHP and reached for the sky as he emerged from the beat-up black hearse, the CHP officers gave him the Rodney King treatment and believed he was on Meth. They had zero tolerance for gunplay and gang violence. A black man in Orange County driving a pimped out hearse and scaring the shit out of all the soccer moms in the community was just asking for a beating. King kept saying he was the victim of a car jacking as they grinded his face into the pavement and kicked him. He remembered a brief moment of bliss, seeing an ice cream truck driving slowly down the street toward him, before the one officer kicked him in the head and rendered him unconscious. King's cell phone was immediately ringing non-stop with illimitable offers from South Central criminal attorneys that had tuned in to the spectacle, screaming police brutality.

He was going to be a rich man after all without the help of *Harold & Maude*.

Agent Kim, now on the scene, first sequestered the purple hearse occupants and the Big Sleep passenger they picked up, and began questioning them about what they were doing in the middle of a heist.

Manfred and Gilda maintained that they drove all the way to Ascension to buy tickets for *Harold and Maude* that was supposed to be screened there that night. It took Agent Kim several minutes to comprehend that they were not referring to the same *Harold & Maude,* but a movie screening of *Harold and Maude.* He questioned them further about Hollywood Forever and "movie night."

Agent Kim noticed that Gilda was wearing a long, black trench coat. He asked where she got it and she replied, "Hollywood Forever." It took another several minutes for Agent Kim to understand that they found the black coat at Hollywood Forever and that someone had left it behind. Gilda also explained that she found the Xerox note for the screening of *Harold & Maude* in the pocket, along with Ray Driscol's, aka Quincy's exhibitor's badge for the Death Expo. She was concerned that she would go to jail for a stolen expo pass and assuming someone else's identity.

Agent Kim examined the photocopy and the badge, putting two and two together ultrafast.

The other officer on the scene spoke with the Big Sleep driver off to the side. He came back and conferred privately with Agent Kim.

They looked back and forth several times at Manfred and Gilda, making them paranoid and often looking serious as hell. Then they would look back at the Big Sleep driver and make him paranoid, whispering back and forth, looking him up and down. Eventually they both laughed and patted each other on the back.

Gilda, Manfred and the Big Sleep driver were put in the back of Agent Kim's car to be taken in for further questioning. He took the long, black trench coat from Gilda before she ducked into the patrol car. Manfred flashed Agent Kim his fangs as they escorted him to the back seat next to her.

Agent Kim lit up a cigarette and leaned against the patrol car. He looked cool with his shades. He was in total control... arriving on the scene... calling all the shots... busting the bad guys. He glanced at Manfred, laughed and imagined the day when Eddie Munster/Manfred would have to grow up and throw away his Halloween costume and get a real job. He pictured Manfred with a name tag at a BestBuy or Target, miserable... being unhelpful with customers and abusing Gilda when he got home. Gilda would eventually leave his ass for a real man.

He lowered his shades and winked at Gilda, thinking "I'm as real as they come baby." Agent Kim said, "I'll see what I can do about that expo pass, maybe get you into some keynote sessions."

Gilda batted her eyelashes at him and looked away from Manfred, who was pissed off that she was flirting.

The patrol car pulled away.

Agent Kim looked at the trench coat in his hands and clutched it like it belonged to him.

Evidence. Handed right to him. It doesn't get much better than that.

He walked back to his car feeling more today like Yun-Fat Chow than ever before.

Chapter **30**

GLADWIN HAD SEVERAL MARTINIS AT THE IVY in Westwood before he returned to his office; it was within walking distance just across Wilshire Boulevard. *The Big Sleep* owner had dropped him off earlier and wished him luck with his investigation. OGR, OCN, and too many trips in hearses drove him back to drinking.

He returned to his desk mid-afternoon. The Amazon box was waiting for him. He ripped the box open expecting to find his Philips Heartstart Home Automated External Defibrillator, but instead he found Jessica Mitford's *The American Way of Death*. He knew the box felt too light. He did not order that book. He checked the packing slip and it was addressed to him. Maybe it was Agent Kim.

He tossed the book aside. He plopped himself down at the desk and once again continued to replay the tapes from *Operation Grim Reaper*.

"Cash at the Y..."

Stop. Rewind. Replay.

"Beautiful bouquet..."

Stop. Rewind. Replay.

This ritual was going nowhere.

He opened up the latest issue of *Men's Health* magazine on his desk. He flipped through the pages, inattentive to the articles. He got up and stretched, gazing out the window that overlooked the gridlock on Wilshire Boulevard. He was bored, drunk and pissed off at this whole Marble City charade.

He stared at the map of cemeteries on his wall and hesitated for a moment, then he began extracting pins from the map. His phone rang. It was Agent Kim.

"G-man?"

"Yeah," Gladwin said, as he cradled the phone with his neck and continued to pull out the pins.

"Where are you, G-man?"

"I'm at the office, Agent Kim... Look I'm kinda busy. Did you locate Stan Glen?" His speech was slightly slurred. He tuned out Agent Kim's response and blurted out, "Son-of-a-bitch!"

"Are you okay, G-Man?" Agent Kim said, wondering if Gladwin finally had a coronary.

Gladwin paused for a moment before responding.

His epiphany left him dumbstruck.

"The little bastard," Gladwin said as he ripped the map off the wall, nearly dropping the phone on the floor.

"Me?" Agent Kim said.

Gladwin did not respond. Agent Kim was fulminating on the other end of the phone.

"Who are you calling a little bastard, sir? Hello? Hello? Are you going to be at the office? I have some additional questions for you."

Gladwin hung up on Agent Kim.

He folded the map and stuffed it in between the pages of the Mitford book, grinning ear to ear. He tucked the book under his arm, hit the elevator and cleared security. His tan Sedan peeled out of the parking lot and hit the 405 Freeway.

Highway 41/46 interchange in Cholame is a historic speck on California's map. It is located between Bakersfield and Paso Robles and is, most notably, the historic crash site where the real, legendary James Dean crashed his silver Porsche Spyder 550 on September 30, 1955. It is *also* know as the "Y."

Gladwin made the journey to the Y in record time, burying the needle to get there. He parked his tan Sedan at the Jack Ranch Café. The café was a combination gift shop, museum and diner all rolled into one, located about 100 yards east of the Y.

Gladwin sat down and observed the tourists inside. The atmosphere was a step back in time; an anachronistic little shop in the middle of nowhere. Immortalized, mythologized and popularized by the death of James Dean.

He ordered some coffee since green tea was not on the menu. The anticipation was killing him. He finally got up after a few cups of black coffee and introduced himself to the owner in back. He flashed his badge and then began asking the usual questions, showing the owner photos of James DeRossa, Stan Glen and the rest of the suspects involved in the attempted *Harold & Maude* heist.

He found out the whole history of the Jack Ranch Café; about the Japanese business man that built it back in 1977 and the stories of all the people, famous and ordinary, that have popped in over the years and paid their respects to James Dean.

Gladwin feigned interest in the owner's anecdotes, but was really only interested in the possibility of *Harold & Maude* being buried somewhere in the vicinity.

He was getting warmer. He could feel it. He asked the owner if he was a movie buff and if he had ever seen the film *Thunderbolt and Lightfoot* with Clint Eastwood and Jeff Bridges. The owner couldn't recall, so Gladwin filled him in on the plot hoping to ring some bells. He explained that, in the film, Eastwood and Bridges pulled off a heist along with George Kennedy. At the end of the film, they find this little schoolhouse where the money is hidden behind the chalkboard.

Gladwin scanned the reaction of the owner's face, hoping to glean a hint of suspicion.

The owner was poker faced.

Gladwin went on about how money could be hiding in other places just like in *Thunderbolt and Lightfoot*. "Take this area for example," he said as he followed the owner into the back. "Out in the boonies. Tourist attraction. Great place to stash money until the heat dies down, right? You get where I'm going?"

The owner finally got wise to Gladwin's Q & A and asked Gladwin, point blank, what the hell he was hinting at. He assured Gladwin there was no money in "them there hills" and walked away from Gladwin to help another tourist in the shop.

Gladwin sat back down at the table, embarrassed. He must've spent another hour and forty-five minutes sitting in the diner.

Waiting.

Gladwin would catch the owner suspiciously staring at him from time to time. He kept his nosed buried in *The American Way of Death* book he brought with him. He also purchased a James Dean bio and pretended to be interested like the other tourists.

Gladwin would glance up from the book and stare out onto the highway and continue to wonder *where* at the Y the money could be. He turned to the back of the book and searched the Index hoping to find further clues.

Another 45 minutes and several cups of coffee passed when Gladwin finally slammed the book shut and bolted out the door.

Chapter **31**

JAMES DEROSSA, AKA "JAMES DEAN" STOOD
in front of Blackwell's Corner peering over his Ray-Bans
as he lit an American Spirit cigarette. Blackwell's Corner
is located in Lost Hills, California, between Highway 46
and 33. It's an old time country store untouched by today's
Wal-Marts. This isolated piece of real estate has a reputation for three things: One: It's known as "the world's
largest parking lot." Two: It has the best pistachios and
almonds. Three: It has the historic reputation of being the
real James Dean's "last stop" before his fatal crash at the Y.
They promote that fact right on the sign in front.

The sun was setting fast. DeRossa nodded politely to the
few remaining people leaving the store. Some townsfolk
talked to DeRossa about the Porsche 550 Spyder replica,
admiring it. DeRossa simply told them that he was a big
fan of the real James Dean and wanted to have the "full"
experience of his historic last stop. A woman asked him if
he was a Hollywood actor and DeRossa politely said "no"

as he removed his Ray-Bans.

After everyone left and night fell, DeRossa popped the trunk and grabbed a duffle bag and a flashlight from inside. He twisted off the top of his Coke, popped a few pistashios and began walking behind the store. It was deserted back there and pitch black.

He caught a coyote in the beam of his flashlight. It dashed off into the night.

He continued to walk about 100 yards into the darkness until his flashlight scanned two 40 foot high Cypress trees peacefully wafting in the cool breeze. They were spread apart by no less than 20 feet. DeRossa moved the beam of light between them like a searchlight from one of those old WWII films. He scanned back and forth three times, left-to-right as a signal.

He moved one step closer to the Cypress trees, when one precise gunshot stopped him dead in his tracks.

The rifle shot came from the direction of an abandoned, dilapidated old barn to the left of the two trees.

Another beam of light emerged moments later, striking the side of DeRossa's right cheek. It was a strong beam— more like a police flashlight.

DeRossa flinched slightly and reached for his Magnum, tucked in a shoulder holster concealed under his mid-length leather.

The sound of boots crunching gravel intensified as the rifleman approached.

"This will be your *last stop* too if you reach for that fucking gun." Detective Gladwin emerged from the dark.

He advised DeRossa to toss the Magnum to his right

and continue walking towards the direction of the two trees.

Dean complied and said, "I was expecting Chuck Conners."

Gladwin didn't laugh and instructed DeRossa in a shaky tone of voice. "This charade is over, pal. You tell me for the last time where Harold and fucking Maude are, or your next trip will be in the back of a hearse."

He kept the rifle trained at the back of DeRossa's neck.

DeRossa didn't say a word. Gladwin cocked the trigger and kept the rifle leveled at DeRossa, waiting. Playtime was over.

At that moment, two headlight beams blasted both of them from between the two Cypress trees.

DeRossa swung around like a heavyweight and clocked Gladwin square in the jaw. The rifle went flying and Gladwin hit the gravel hard, landing flat on his back.

Gladwin felt DeRossa might have broken his jaw.

DeRossa picked up Gladwin's rifle and pointed it right at Gladwin's heart.

Gladwin lost consciousness and passed out cold.

The next morning, Gladwin woke to the sound of a rooster and Agent Kim hovering over him, flanked by two LA sheriffs. The sun was rising over the hills. They helped him to his feet and walked him back into Blackwell's Corner to get him some black coffee.

The first words out of Gladwin's mouth, after a few sips of coffee, was: "Dean and his thugs did this to me."

A tourist buying a postcard from the rack tuned into the the name "Dean" and assumed they were talking about the real James Dean, but that wouldn't make any sense, so the tourist assumed that Gladwin was crazy and the officers were there to arrest him.

Agent Kim and the sheriffs stood by observing Gladwin. He was still disoriented by the blow to the head.

Gladwin finally laughed uncomfortably in between sips and said, "Jesus, you guys look like you just came back from a funeral."

Agent Kim stood there with his shades on, cocky as hell. He chewed a toothpick, devoid of expression, posturing his best Yun-Fat Chow.

Gladwin said, "What are you guys doing down here anyway? What day is it? I thought I was pretty clear on you maintaining your position in OC."

Agent Kim looked around the grocery store, rolling the toothpick in his mouth and finally said, "How did you wind up all the way down here, G-man?"

Gladwin looked around the grocery store, modulating his voice to a loud whisper, "Crash at the Y, is cash at the Y... I figured it out. Cholame means beautiful bouquet... Dean died in 55... it all adds up."

The tourist moved in closer to eavesdrop, hoping to glean more facts on the James Dean crash site. Gladwin flashed him a dirty look.

Agent Kim stood there expressionless.

"Don't you see," Gladwin said, "the money is buried out there." He pointed across the highway. The agents followed his finger and then continued to stare him down.

"Ah, where," Agent Kim said with a sarcastic undertone.

"How the hell do I know, I was sandbagged. I remember

being worked over by Dean. He must've taken the money and hit the road in his Spyder."

The tourist let out a laugh and turned his back on Gladwin and the sheriffs. He continued to look at postcards on the rack.

Agent Kim and the other agents were smirking at Gladwin.

"So you think Dean fit *Harold & Maude* in that little silver Spyder and is heading for the border?

"Don't patronize me."

"Follow us, G-man," Agent Kim said. "I have a few items in my car you might be interested in."

Gladwin hesitated a moment, then walked outside to the black, unmarked car. He slid in the passenger side. The sheriffs got in the back seat. Before Agent Kim got in, he popped the trunk and took out a brown evidence bag and got into the driver's side. Gladwin glanced at the brown bag and wondered what clue Agent Kim might have found to *Harold & Maude*.

Agent Kim said, "Were you at Hollywood Forever two nights ago?"

Gladwin thought hard for a moment.

"Yes, I had some additional questions for the staff there. I was following up on a few leads."

"Where'd you go before that?" Agent Kim said.

"I surveillanced Dean at the Roosevelt."

Gladwin had interrogated many suspects over the course of his career and did not appreciate the tables being turned on him, particularly by a hot shot punk like Agent Kim.

Gladwin said, "Hey, what the hell is this anyway?"

One of the sheriffs barked back at him and advised him to just answer the question.

Agent Kim said, "Where did DeRossa go?"

"Egyptian Theatre in Hollywood."

"Did you go to the Egyptian Theatre that night?"

"No," Gladwin said, "my investigation ended there."

"Why?"

"Whadda you mean, why?" Gladwin said. He really wanted to take Agent Kim's smug head off. "Because, Agent Kim, I was over at Hollywood Forever asking more questions."

"What was the movie that was playing at the cemetery?"

"I don't know. I think Rebel Without A Cause." Gladwin thought about the irony of it all and the absurdity of 'movie night' at Hollywood Forever. "Can you believe that people actually show up in a cemetery to watch a movie? It looked sold out that night."

"Well G-man, I was at the movies myself that night," Agent Kim said.

"You were at the Egyptian?"

"Not quite. I was watching the streets of Hollywood."

Gladwin didn't understand where Agent Kim was going with his annoying questions.

"Is that a film?" Gladwin said and subsequently laughed.

"Yes, and it features you."

"Come again."

"I do love the Patriot Act, Detective Gladwin," Agent Kim said, as he removed his shades and reached into the bag. "We watched you go into a parking garage that night via an electric eye on Hollywood Boulevard. He opened the brown evidence bag and pulled a large, sealed plastic bag with Quincy's black trench coat. "You recognize this trench coat?"

"Should I?" Gladwin lied.

"How about this?" Agent Kim pulled out the black Memorial Guest Registry book sealed in another plastic evidence bag. "This was returned to us with a Hollywood Forever 'movie night' ticket inside the book. It was found in the Big Sleep hearse you jacked— the owner returned it to me at the office because he thought it belonged to you."

Gladwin looked away.

"We found Quincy murdered in the parking garage."

"Do you have that on tape?" Gladwin said.

"Don't need it. You left us enough incriminating evidence to work with." He tossed Quincy's exhibitor badge on Gladwin's lap. Gladwin was shitting bricks and became flush in the face. He shifted in his seat.

"Where'd that come from?"

"You."

"Me."

"Yes, you," Agent Kim said, "after you killed Ray Driscol you ditched his black trench coat."

"You have a witness?"

"Yes, we have witnesses that saw you ditch Driscol's trench coat at Hollywood Forever."

Gladwin sat silent, staring out the window for several minutes. He knew they had him by the balls. He finally said, "*Harold & Maude...*"

Agent Kim and the sheriffs did not say a word.

"What about DeRossa? Stan Glen?"

"We'll take over from here. We'll continue the investigation and close it."

Gladwin had thrown away a prestigious career. Over what? A sham? He had seen other officers, councilmen, judges and attorneys get caught up in corruption over the course of his career, but he always felt it wouldn't happen to him. He hung his head down, ashamed and angry. Driving that silver Big Sleep hearse downhill from the Hollywood sign popped into his mind again. He thought about celebrity death and people like OJ, Robert Blake, Phil Spector and all the scandal that comes with a situation like this. He was no celebrity, but the media was about to descend on him. He got caught up in someone else's movie and now he was going to do time.

They booked him on: murder, stolen property, misuse of departmental funds and tampering with evidence. One sheriff got out and drove Gladwin's car back to LA. The other stayed to oversee Gladwin. Agent Kim lit up a cigarette and stayed behind as they hit highway.

The tourist emerged from the Blackwell grocery store, followed by a few other looky-loos. They asked him if he knew what happened. The tourist explained that the man they arrested was crazy and thought that James Dean had attacked him.

Chapter **32**

AGENT KIM WAITED FOR STAN GLEN INSIDE the Jack Ranch Café. Glen was over half-an-hour late.

"What took you?" Agent Kim said.

"What else," Stan Glen said, "traffic."

Agent Kim pushed the morning paper across the table. The headlines read: *High Speed Funeral Procession Culminates in Deadly Ending In Orange County."*

"It was a bloodbath," Agent Kim said, observing the dumbstruck look on Glen's face.

Stan Glen shifted in his seat and said, "Well, other people sorta got in the way."

"Other people got killed. That wasn't part of the sting."

Glen pushed the paper aside and stared outside at the silver James Dean memorial gleaming in the sun and finally said, "Where is Dean?"

"We're tracing him. Let's go back to the tapes."

"Look, Agent Kim, we went over this before."

"That was before you got here. Things changed, so let's go over it again."

Stan Glen sighed and said, "I'm supposed to be enjoying my retirement here."

"You've had enough sun, that's why we sprung you from retirement, not to mention we turned a blind eye to you posing as Maple," Agent Kim said. "You're not going to take any more cruises on my department's dime if we don't start making some progress in this sting. Am I making sense?" Agent Kim kept staring at Glen and said, "You got something solid I can take to the DA or not on DeRossa... Hoffa... anything?"

"Okay look," Stan Glen leaned across the table and lowered his voice to a whisper, "Dean got a visit from Ray Driscol, the man you know as Quincy—"

"Knew as Quincy."

"Knew?"

"Yeah, Gladwin killed him. Move on with your story."

Quincy's death threw a wrench into Glen's concentration. After several seconds he finally said, "So, ah where was I... Ohh, like I was telling you, so DeRossa got a visit from Quincy a few months prior to his parole—" Glen lost his train of thought, "Did Gladwin get the Memorial Guest Registry book from Dean?"

"Yeah, Dean gave him the slip. It's a fake."

"No, the real one is still out there. Dean has it."

"Prove it."

"We've seen it."

"You're the only person left alive from that night."

"Quincy was there the night DeRossa's father was murdered. He was our informant. Like I've already told you, he was the attendee that was ejected who was working with the Feds and Maple and I during OGR—"

"Why was Big Frank murdered?"

"Why else, the money."

"Cut to the chase... where is the money?"

"At the Y."

"We're here," Agent Kim looked around the cafe and said, "and it ain't here."

"Well then, there has to be another Y."

"We're running out of them."

"I can't believe you guys lost Dean."

"We're running out of options at this point. We want you to meet with Dean."

"C'mon on. I can't do that... you know that. He knows who I am."

"Then he'll know that you're helping us heat a cold case. What are you so afraid of?"

"You're sending me for a ride in the back of a hearse. This guy still paints houses."

Agent Kim laughed, "What the hell does that mean?"

"It means to 'kill a man' in mafia lingo. Didn't you learn anything from the Hoffa tapes? These guys don't fuck around."

"The mafia is as dead as Dean... you expect me to buy into your ancient fears?"

"Send someone else on a deathride, not me."

"We got your back."

Agent Kim looked him square in the eye, "You were brought in to help us nail Dean. Instead, we somehow got my boss on murder charges and a misguided mess to clean up in Orange County."

"Hey, no one asked Gladwin to kill Quincy. He fucked himself."

"So now that leaves you."

"That leaves me what?"

"That leaves you to fix it."

"What about Bishop and King?"

"King was taken into custody..." Agent Kim hesitated a moment and continued, "Bishop was murdered. Never made it to the party. Gang related."

"Dead?"

"S'what I said... 99 & 44/100% d-e-a-d."

"Bishop wasn't involved in any gang activity."

Agent Kim opened Cash Worthington's dead g-ster scrapbook of Poloroids and flipped to the photo of the now deceased Wes Bishop with four bullets in his chest. He said, "Well, he somehow got involved."

"Doesn't make any sense."

"It doesn't have to at this point. The gangster dude's name was Cash Worthington."

"The infomercial guy that sells cars?"

"No, that's Cal Worthington," Agent Kim said. "Cash Worthington just got out of jail for a B & E at a local liquor store. He murdered Bishop and their dog at their mortuary. We're trying to sort it all out."

Stan Glen was deep in thought, then he blurted out, "What kind of dog was it?"

"What?"

"The dog that got killed."

"A Pit. It was one of those Pit Bulls."

"Hate those dogs."

"Let's get off the dog talk."

"It sounds to me like King was the one involved with the gangsters. Maybe he was out to burn Bishop and take the money."

"Sounds like a lot of things. A lot of things that don't sound right," Agent Kim said.

"All right, so I'll meet with Dean. Is that what you want?"

"You know what I want."

"Yeah, I know what you want."

"You know where to find him?"

"C'mon Agent Kim, I was a detective, remember?"

Stan Glen stared into space for a few minutes, reflecting on concerns that only he would be concerned about and Agent Kim would never understand in a million years. He said, "Okay, so then we play it my way. I can't wear a wire, he'll know."

"No wire then."

"It's strictly off the record."

"Sure."

"How are you going to get anything to stick?"

"Let us worry about that. Just have the conversation with Dean."

"What conversation is that?"

"Whatever conversation you've been avoiding."

"Like the conversations that aren't on those tapes?"

"Yeah, like those kinds of conversations."

Stan Glen stirred his coffee, ruminating on his fate.

"You have me covered on this deal?"

"We always take care of our own."

Agent Kim studied Glen's face and attempted to break the somber mood. He said, "Hey, c'mon, the mob is history... you act like this guy is Gotti." He laughed when he thought about Detective Gladwin opening the gold urn that Stan Glen brought with him. He said, "You should have seen Gladwin's face when he thought you were ashes... I mean, he was speechless."

Stan Glen sat at the table with no expression on his face, reflecting on the urn filled with cigarette butts. He was speechless.

Stan Glen observed Dean for several moments before approaching him at the Dakota restaurant in the Hollywood Roosevelt. Most of the tables were vacant. Dean sat in the back of the restaurant, working on an LA Times crossword puzzle, when Glen sat down across from him. Dean did not flinch. He smiled.

"Do you know who I am?" Stan Glen said.

"Yes, I know exactly who you are."

"Do you know why I'm here?"

"Yes, and I also know why you are not here."

"Good. Then knowing all those whys will save us both a lot of time."

The Dakota waitress brought Stan Glen a menu. He said he was just there to have coffee. The waitress brought him some and refilled Dean's cup.

Dean pulled out Stan Glen's report from OGR. He pushed the report across the table under Glen's nose. Glen glanced at it superficially.

"There was something about your report that always bothered me," Dean said.

"And what's that?"

"Why I'm standing here today... alive."

"You were damn lucky, that's all. Your guardian angel must've been watching over you."

"I wouldn't exactly call you my guardian angel."

"What's that supposed to mean?" Glen had a vacant look on his face.

"I was kept alive for a reason," Dean said. "Quincy planted that bomb and you detonated it."

"That's insane. You and I both know Mike Maple and Quincy were behind your father's death. They were selling guns to both sides and they got theirs. Your father can finally rest in peace."

Dean pulled out the jaundiced PennyPress magazine from that night.

"You didn't count on me taking a ride with my father... none of you did. But you would've killed him just the same, eventually in cold blood over the money. Only you knew I had the secret to OGR. When I went back in the funeral home to retrieve my magazine, you guys got my father out of the way first. After he was killed, I guess you figured it would be like stealing candy from a baby? Only the Feds kept getting in the way. Someone was always breathing down your necks."

"Look DeRossa, Quincy is dead," Stan Glen said.

"Good, that saves me the trouble of doing it myself and pinning it on you. So, why did you kill him?"

Stan Glen laughed and said, "I didn't, that deranged detective did."

"I'm not talking about Quincy, I'm talking about my father."

"Mike Maple murdered your father."

"Then who killed Mike Maple."

"Who else... the mob."

"Bullshit."

"Well it doesn't much matter whether it's bullshit or not. Mike Maple sorta got in the way and so have you." Stan Glen flashed a small revolver from his windbreaker and said, "I'm hoping you don't make the same mistake. We both have our dirty little secrets."

"Like?"

"Like Hoffa's disappearance— the whole reason we were there that night at your father's funeral home. If he'd kept his nose clean in the first place, he might be sittin' here with you today drinking coffee. Big Frank cremated him."

"No. Pete Vital disposed of Hoffa with his incinerator, and you know it. Hoffa shoulda known better than to get into a car with those guys– with any guys for that matter. He trusted 'em and they killed him."

"Yeah well, your father played a hand in it, so it's hard for me to get all misty about your loss." Stan Glen finished his coffee and said, "So since you know all the whys to everything, why don't you tell me which Y the loot is buried at."

Dean opened up the PennyPress magazine and began to

decipher a cryptogram located on one of the yellowed pages. The handwriting was not his own but that of his fathers. It read:

bmoys ogy wrpxy yutb
but ogy axv bgrl xb rpys,
b syayi bgrqit wbey bwyutb
but oqsu ogy iybm rpys.

Stan Glen watched him decipher the code, glancing up occasionally at Dean, amazed at how quickly his mind was working. Dean spun the magazine around and pushed it forward to Glen. It read:

After the movie ends
and the big show is over,
a rebel must make amends
and turn the leaf over.

Stan Glen said, "What the hell is that supposed to mean? Is it a poem?"

"*Harold & Maude* is done. The big show is over."

"Look, I don't have any more time for some goddamn DaVinci code game. Spell it out for me."

"There is no Memorial Guest Registry book. This is it."

Glen stared at the cryptogram. Dumbstruck.

"You better start making some sense."

"My father passed this to me before you killed him."

"I said I didn't kill him."

"Whatever."

"My father was a big fan of the real James Dean. *Rebel Without a Cause* was one of his all time favorites. I showed up here, out of respect for my father, to make amends and turn over a new leaf."

"That's it? You expect me to believe that?"

"No. There's more of course. There is another Y, as you guessed."

Glen slapped his hand on the table and said, "I knew it!"

"Have you heard of a place called Keddie?"

"No."

"It's located up in California. Not too far from Reno... actually about 90 miles away."

"Go on."

"It's a place called the Keddie Wye." Dean drew a triangle on a white napkin and explained. "The railroad industry uses the wye to turn trains around. North America has more wyes than anywhere else. Anyway, they built this miraculous wye on two tall trestles that rise to high elevation above the rocky chasm of the Feather River.

"So it's under that wye? How do we get to it?"

"No. It's near that wye in Spanish Creek. There is a yellow Tudor cottage that an undertaker friend of my father's owned. He lived in Reno and kept it under his name for him. My father used to take Josephine Franzetta up there before his divorce."

"The broad from Windsor Racetrack."

"That was her. As I said, the Keddie Wye is only about 90 minutes from Reno. Back in 1974, two airtrays left Toronto on two flights with the stolen money from Windsor Racetrack and the diamonds from the port. However, it was not a non-stop flight. They landed in Reno, which was never documented, and *Harold & Maude* as they came to be known, took a train from Reno to the Keddie Wye. The cover story was that they were headed to a local funeral home in Spanish Creek, but the two airtrays never made it to that funeral home. Instead, the hearse took a detour and delivered them to the tudor in Spanish Creek. The diamonds and money were then stored inside the walls of the small three bedroom house for safekeeping."

Stan Glen sat there for some time staring into his black coffee. It all seemed to make sense. You couldn't make this stuff up, as they say. He was about to hit pay dirt. Endless Carnival Cruises anywhere in the world. He said, "I think it's time for you and I to take a little drive and finalize this transaction, once and for all."

"Sorry Stan. I don't get into cars with people I don't trust. And even if I did trust you, I still wouldn't get in a car with you."

"Well then, give me the directions and I'll meet you there."

"It's going to be a long ride."

"It's been a long enough ride already."

"Did you drive here?"

"I have a rental car."

"You were followed."

"Without a doubt. Gladwin's associate is tailing me, I'm playing him though. I can shake him."

"I can't take that kind of a chance."

Stan Glen didn't say a word. He was out of options.

"Well, what are we going to do, just sit here and stare at each other all day."

Dean looked out the window of the Dakota, watching the valets run back and forth parking cars.

"Tell you what. Leave the rental car and meet me out front in five minutes."

"Then what?"

"I'll have someone else pick us up."

Stan Glen sat back in his seat and laughed. "What do you take me for?"

"A fool?"

"Yeah, that's what I thought you took me for. You had me going with this cock-and-bull story about the Keddie Wye and now I'm supposed to just get in a car with you so that you can blow my brains out?"

"I'm going down to the Keddie Wye in less than five minutes, with or without you, so it doesn't much matter what you think."

Dean got up and started walking in the opposite direction of the valet entrance and towards the front entrance on Hollywood Boulevard.

Stan Glen got up and followed him. He caught up to Dean and jabbed the gun through his windbreaker into Dean's right rib before they were about to exit onto Hollywood Boulevard. Glen said, "I'll call us a cab and you can pick up the fucking tab. That's how we'll play it. If your story turns out to be a lie, then you can join your father."

Glen was about to call a cab on his cell phone when Dean said, "You are a fool. Hang up the cell phone and shut it off. Why not just give the agents the number of

Yellow Cab and have them call it for you? Think about it."

Glen thought about it. Dean was right. He felt stupid.

Glen nudged Dean out onto Hollywood Boulevard. It was crowded with tourists. Glen hailed the first yellow cab he could.

The yellow cab was about to stop when a white van cut in front of it and layed on it's horn, causing an outbreak of apparent road rage. The side door flung open on the white van and Glen felt another nudge from behind. There was a gun at his back. Coffin Joe forced him into the white van and Dean closed the sliding door behind them both.

Daisy Acres was in the driver's seat and hauled ass back out onto Hollywood Boulevard.

Dean twisted the revolver out of Glen's hand, tossing him to the other side. The van made a sharp turn onto the 101 Freeway. Glen was all turned around. Disoriented. He looked at Dean and then back at Coffin Joe with the gun trained on him, and then at Daisy Acres' eyes in the rearview mirror.

"Where are you taking me?"

"Just shut up and enjoy the ride," Dean said. Dean climbed into the passenger seat next to Daisy Acres and said, "You'll eventually need to get on the I-80 South, Josephine."

Glen studied the eyes in the rearview mirror. "You're Josephine Franzetta," he said. He glanced back at Coffin Joe who kept the gun on Glen.

Josephine kept her eyes on the road and did not acknowledge Glen's epiphany.

Dean turned around and kept the gun on Glen as Coffin Joe peeled off the bushy mustache, along with the mop of hair and chauffeur's cap. She tossed her flowing blonde hair Rita Hayworth style and smiled. She was a knockout.

Dean smiled and said, "And this is my sister, Jackie."

Glen looked down at the scratched up steel floor in the van. He looked back at the numerous floral arrangements in the rear that were out for delivery. A bouquet of sunflowers caught his attention. He turned his attention to Jackie and said, "So you're Big Frank's love child?"

It was obvious and did not require a response or confirmation from anyone else in the van.

Dean threw an old black Memorial Guest Registry book in front of Stan Glen. Glen picked it up and looked at.

"Go ahead. Open it."

Glen opened the black Memorial Guest Registry book.

"Open it to the gold leaf in the middle."

Glen did as he was asked and studied the names.

"You see anybody you know?"

Glen looked at the following names:

James Dean
Mr. Blackwell

"Who is Mr. Blackwell?"

"No one. Mr. Blackwell was referring to Blackwell's Corner."

"But I was there... with the agent... the money wasn't

there."

"The money was there before you got there."

"And so were we," Jackie said.

Daisy Acres said, "That Detective Gladwin figured it out and followed us there."

"That was until my brother knocked his lights out," Jackie said.

"The money was at the Y all along. The surveillance tapes were—"

"— were right." Stan Glen said. His mind flashed to the tapes from "Operation Grim Reaper." The words echoed: *"Tutor... beautiful bouquet... Cash at the Y and 55."* He saw the reels of tape turn slowly. Those phrases repeating over and over again. He glanced back at the sunflowers once more, and then back at Dean.

"So I was hoping that you would confess to our father's murder," Dean said.

Glen did not confess or say another word. He just kept staring at the sunflowers gently bouncing in the back of the white van, occasionally catching a ray of light. Resplendent.

Dean lit up an American Spirit cigarette. He took a long drag and exhaled the smoke in Glen's direction. He said, "You know, I think the trick to this life is knowing which car not to get into." He instructed Josephine to keep heading towards the direction of Reno to connect with his father's undertaker friend who owed him a favor.

Chapter **33**

AGENT KIM COULD NOT REACH STAN GLEN
on his cell phone or in his room at the W Hotel in West-wood. It had been two days. He located his Hertz rental car at the Hollywood Roosevelt. It was a green Ford Focus. Empty. Nothing left behind that would indicate a struggle. He interviewed the waitress at the Dakota and she did acknowledge serving James DeRossa and Stan Glen, and positively identified them in photos. She stated that the taller, good looking gentleman got up from the table and walked away from the older gentleman. He appeared to be annoyed by him, and in her opinion, the older gentleman had a "jerky" attitude.

Agent Kim was not interested in her opinion. She informed him that they went in the direction of the front of the hotel, out to Hollywood. Agent Kim thanked her for her time and walked outside the Hollywood Roosevelt in that direction. He looked up and down Hollywood Boulevard and at the passing tourists. He asked around the local shops to see if anyone observed anything out of the ordinary, and most store owners told him that everything they see is out of the ordinary on Hollywood Boulevard. Agent Kim, running short on patience, then would ask them again if they had seen anything ordinary then. Nobody had seen anything. This always amazed Agent Kim as a detective. Shouldn't more people pay attention to their surroundings?

He checked back with the hotel manager, Javier, and asked if the Roosevelt had any security cameras. Javier said only on the inside. None outside.

Agent Kim placed a call to the Hollywood police department and asked if they had an electric eye on that section of the boulevard near the Roosevelt. That area unfortunately was not covered, according to the detective he spoke with. He did not trust Stan Glen as far as he could spit and wondered if he and Dean had been working together all along. He went back outside on Hollywood Boulevard and lit up a cigarette. He kicked his leg back against a shop wall and watched the dregs of Hollywood pass by on skateboards and worn out Sketchers. Bald shining heads, gangsta wannabes and the occasional Mohawk. He finished his smoke, flicked it on the cement across Patty Duke's star and headed back to the office.

Agent Kim continued to follow up on some leads that Gladwin had developed. His first stop was *The Big Sleep Celebrity Death Tours*. He interviewed the owner and the owner reiterated what he had already told Detective Gladwin. The only person that was unaccounted for was Jackie Antos, aka "Coffin Joe." Agent Kim put another detective

on her, but that detective turned up zip on her whereabouts or her real identity. The owner also went on to
explain that it's hard to find hearse drivers, even in Hollywood. He pointed out his newest hire. Agent Kim
looked in the direction of a gothic punk polishing a silver
hearse.

He took a double take.

It was Manfred O.

On that note, Agent Kim just shook his head and returned to the FBI field office.

When he got back in the office, he noticed a large bouquet of sunflowers sitting in the middle of his desk. His
mind flashed to Manfred's sexy girlfriend, Gilda. Maybe
she did look him up, after all, and dumped Bela Lugosi.

He raced over to the bouquet and plucked the note card
off the base. The small envelope contained a mailbox key
and a box number, along with the business card of the
Mailboxes Etc. It was the same location that he had been
to before.

He drove up Westwood Boulevard and pulled into the
underground parking structure located on Le Conte. He
entered the Mail Boxes Etc. place. He located box # 407.
He opened the mailbox and pulled out a large package
from inside.

When he got in the car he ripped open the package. It
contained a Payless shoe box taped shut. Agent Kim hesitated for a moment and then sliced opened the tape on
the box, using his keys. He grimaced. It was a gold urn.

Stan Glen was ashes. James DeRossa had settled the score.

He diverted his gaze from the urn to the wall in the parking garage. The wall was tagged and sprayed with blue gang graffiti. He reflected on Bishop and King's black hearse tagged with gang graffiti. He lit up another cigarette and stared at the wall in front of his car for several minutes. He ruminated on the old school mafia. Jimmy Hoffa. John Gotti. How LA has a new breed of gangsters and their disparities— The mafia didn't need to advertise on walls. They just took care of business. Fuckers, he thought. All of 'em. He glanced back down at the urn and snuffed his cigarette out inside. He would file an affidavit for an arrest warrant on James DeRossa for the murder of Stan Glen when he returned to the office.

He threw the car in reverse and headed back out of the underground parking garage and back out onto Le Conte.

At the same time, James DeRossa took the ticket issued by an airline representative at the counter in Reno. 7:45 p.m. departure back to Detroit. He looked at the name issued on the ticket: *Marlon Brando*.

As he boarded, the young clerk smiled and said, "Have a great flight, Mr. Brando."

So much for Homeland Security. Cat Steven's song *Wild World* from *Harold and Maude* popped into his head. DeRossa smiled back at the clerk and walked down the jetway.

ॐ

Acknowledgments

Thank you to the Shores Madrid— my Cinema Paradiso; Elaine Naughton, who never censored what I read, watched or joked about, and of course, engendered an overactive imagination; The memory of Dave "Mad Dog" McDowell, and my sister Michelle—You made it through the San Bernardino Mountains! The whole Naughton clan, Mike and Sharon Martino, and Tom and Dorothy Rose for their unending support; Borders; Jorge Garcia, who hit the lotto... big time! Amazon.com; "M" & "Z" who made me realize a six-figure potential. Michael Madsen and "Ma Barker" for giving me the opportunity and trusting me. Quentin Tarantino. Rod Serling and Willoughby. My wife Donna, who was responsible for getting this mystery on the road and has seen me through the 10 year journey when this novel was originally written as a script, and to Zuko— writer's friend, and quite possibly the greatest dog that has ever lived!

— Beverly Hills, California
April 12th, 2008